AUGUST

GABI SALAS

Paperback ISBN: 979-8-9889056-2-2

For all my spooky, slutty girlies

TROPES, TAGS, AND TRIGGER WARNINGS

Tropes:

Paranormal, psychics, fated love, reverse harem (kinda)

Tags:

Magic, gothic, immortality, goth girl, good guy, haunted mansion, urban fantasy

Trigger Warnings:

This book uses explicit language and very descriptive sex scenes. There is a very mild element of death (not graphic). There is a non-human sexual element.

I love him not for the way he silenced my demons,
but for the way his demons dance with mine.

HARLEY QUINN

ONE

SUNDAY

"Maybe this headache will finally be the thing to kill me." Sunday Strange's humor wasn't received well by the rest of the family.

"Don't be so morbid, dear, we haven't even had dessert yet," her mother, Tish, spoke warmly from the other end of the long, wooden table. A feast sat between them, as it did every night.

Sunday narrowed her eyes and gripped the silverware in her hands as another vision squeezed her brain. The last few months, the visions had all been the same. They always started with a large bang—jolting her awake or stealing her attention from whatever she was doing—then flashes of light, metal crunching, a tree, and then. . . nothing. The vision would stop just as the tree came into view. Something about the tree's bark was familiar, but Sunday hadn't placed it yet.

She had been getting psychic visions and hallucinations

as far back as she could remember. Her mother called her The Raven because Sunday's visions were always dark. They foresaw depression, pain, death, and other morbid fascinations from both the past and the future. Tish, her mother, and her mother's mother all had the same ability, albeit slightly less depressing. However, Sunday had learned that, with practice, she could hone her visions into being helpful.

Because the darkness didn't bother Sunday. Instead, the darkness called to her, making her body tingle and her brain quiet in curiosity. However, she wondered if the darkness would drag her under and not allow her to resurface once and for all.

Grandmama scooped a ladle of pumpkin soup into the bowl in front of Sunday and the nutmeg and cinnamon wafting up to her nose eased the headache slightly. The visions always came with dizziness and left her with a massive headache that made her want to sleep for days. Tonight would be no different. Tonight, perhaps Cosa could help ease her into a deeper sleep, so maybe the vision wouldn't wake her again before morning.

As if it heard her thoughts, Cosa scuttled across the tabletop and stood next to her plate. The townspeople may consider the inhabitants of the Strange family home to be odd characters, but to Sunday, they were family. Cosa had come into her life two years ago as a souvenir from her father's work travels. It knew what she needed, sometimes even before she did, and it was always happy to provide.

Sunday took a deep breath and stared down at the swirly orange liquid in her bowl. Her stomach growled, but her head made her sway. Before she could even will her hands to lift from the table, Cosa took it upon itself to do the work for her. It wrapped its thick fingers around the spoon to the side of the bowl and dipped it in, scooping up a steamy serving.

Cosa brought it to her mouth, she opened her lips, and in the spoon went. It seemed to enjoy feeding her. Not that Sunday could ever know for sure since it couldn't speak. In fact, Cosa was just a hand. It walked on the tips of its fingers and scurried around the house as it pleased. Cosa didn't always need a surface in order to move around. Sunday had been surprised the first time it'd come up into her bathroom as she was getting ready one morning. She had watched in the mirror as it floated in the air behind her and fingered her hair into tight braids.

Cosa brought another spoonful of soup to her mouth, and her lips obeyed as they opened to allow the liquid inside to warm her belly. She sat quietly at the table as Cosa continued to feed her, and her family chatted about town events. Sunday was as young as seven when she realized that her family vastly differed from other families.

It turns out that other families don't have a grandfather who enjoys sleeping in a silk-lined coffin at night or a father who travels the world collecting relics of asylums and abandoned carnivals. Other people's families' favorite colors weren't black, nor do they use elemental magic to clean their homes. The Strange family ancestors have always lived in plain sight of regular people, so Sunday knew other families existed and knew, precisely, what made hers different.

Sunday had mostly avoided the outside world, having

deemed them "too full of life" for her taste. She'd insisted on being homeschooled and had transitioned right into college-level classes as soon as she'd passed secondary school two years ago.

Last year, at eighteen, she started using her skills under a pseudonym when she found online forums of unsolved cases. Although Sunday hadn't quite figured out how to summon her visions specifically, she could guide them. If she could focus on a particular case, usually after devouring every file she could hack into from various police departments, her next vision would serve her up a nugget of information.

Sometimes, it would be the name of a person or a business; other times, it would be a vision of fabric or the furniture in a room. Sunday would sketch what she saw and compare her notes to the case files until something clicked. Then, she'd anonymously submit her tip to the correct department and leave the rest to the detectives. When she came across a headline in a newspaper about how a thirty-seven-year-old case was solved thanks to a nameless tip, she allowed a rare smile.

Now, cases piled high in her room, along with books on forensics, blood analysis, and body decomposition stacked high on her dresser. Sunday's life wasn't like other nineteen-year-old girls' lives, but those girls had more significant problems than she ever wanted to deal with. They had to deal with *living people*.

She was content living in her family's spooky Victorian mansion that sat high on a hill above a cemetery and a swamp with her grandparents, parents, brother, cousin, butler, and

Cosa until the day she died. She was content, because, well, Sunday was never *happy* anywhere or with anyone.

But that was the other thing: Sunday hadn't yet told her parents about the vision she'd gotten last week. The one that showed *her* future. The future that never ended.

There had been rumors inside her family for years about how, every few decades, a few family members were deemed worthy of being immortal. Sunday had first heard this rumor when her cousin Itta came to live with them when she was only twelve. Apparently, Itta had been chosen to be one of the immortal ones and figured she might as well spend some of her time getting to know Sunday and her parents before she moved on to somewhere else.

Sunday hoped she wouldn't. Although she lacked the words to describe how she felt, she kind of thought that she might *like* Itta. Itta had taken it upon herself to act as a big sister to Sunday, and since Itta was perpetually twenty-seven, Sunday still had eight more years for that to be true.

A loud bang caused Sunday to gasp, and Cosa dropped the spoon as it hung halfway to her lips. All eyes at the table flew to her, and she groaned at the attention. It was the vision again. Sunday scooted her chair away from the table and, without a word, turned to head up to her section of the house.

This mansion had been in the Strange family since the late 1800s, and the wealth from the oil that had been found underneath it kept her family comfortable. The townspeople wanted to tear it down and parcel off the land for developments. They hated that her family benefited richly from its spot. And that pleased Sunday.

Sunday climbed the broad staircase to the third floor, her hand running over the glossy wooden railing, her footsteps muffled by the Persian runner covering each step. Her large, wooden door heaved closed behind her on its own as she stepped inside her bedroom. Sunday ignored the piles of papers of unsolved cases on her desk and instead headed straight to the plush bed waiting for her.

Unlike her grandfather, Sunday preferred to sleep in a bed that could swallow you with all its softness and billowy pillows. Every night, she nested herself in the middle, pillows piled high all around her and dark curtains drawn around the four posters of her bed. Sunday slipped off her tight black dress, leaving it in a heap at the side of her bed. By morning, the house's magic would pick it up. The magic was a clean freak.

Sunday slipped her panties down next, climbing into the bed bare. She liked the feel of the coolness of the sheets against her skin. Any fabric between her and them would only make her overheat. Her head lay down on the pillows behind her as she heard the squeak of the brass knob at her door turn.

Cosa.

Sunday slept with warm candles flickering all around her room, so there was a soft glow even with the dark curtains closed. She knew without *really* knowing that the magic of the house would keep the place from burning to the ground. Not that it wouldn't be cool to see. Sunday felt a soft thump on the mattress as Cosa made its way up. She took a deep breath and sighed into the darkness.

Cosa journeyed up to her pillow and massaged her scalp, and tension from the latest vision released its grip. The last vision had shown something new. A flash of red. A swatch of denim. A flurry of brown curls. And then nothing. Sunday didn't know if it had already happened or was about to happen or who it involved.

Sunday sighed as Cosa trailed a finger down her cheek and ran it loosely over her bottom lip. Her chin dropped open automatically as Cosa slid two fingers past her teeth and into the warmth of her mouth. She sucked on its fingers, tasting a little of the pumpkin soup from dinner. With wet fingers, Cosa made a trail down her throat and between her breasts, circling each nipple, causing them to peak from the cold. She sunk further into the bed, giving Cosa permission to continue.

And it did. After roughly tugging on both nipples, Cosa walked its fingers down her belly and slid its pointer finger down her already wet middle. Sunday pulled her knees up and widened her legs, and Cosa rewarded her by dipping one finger inside. She leaned up on her elbows to watch as this hand dipped in and out of her.

Another finger was added, and Sunday's breath picked up. Cosa's fingers were *thick*, larger than most human hands. Sunday didn't know if this hand ever belonged to an actual body before or if this was always the state it'd been in. Her father, Castillo, had found it in some occult shop in Spain a couple of years ago and had to have it.

Last year, Sunday had been in bed with one of her favorite vibrators when the batteries went out right before she could orgasm. She huffed and tossed it against the wall, watching it shatter to pieces. Cosa had opened her door then, and she had hurried to cover herself. Not that she should; it had been in *her* bedroom. But it had climbed up on the bed, tugged the sheet down for her, and nudged her to lie back down. So, she had.

Cosa had ended up finger fucking her into three orgasms that night. It was now her trusty accessory in coming. Sometimes, it used its own fingers; other times, it held toys for her. But no matter what, she knew, without fail, that she would explode soon. Cosa helped her relax. It calmed her down from the visions and was the only thing that let her get any remnants of sleep at night.

And Sunday was hooked. One look at Cosa, and it knew what she wanted, and it was always happy to oblige. Sometimes, she would zone out at breakfast, the sounds of her mother's soft voice going on in the background, and Sunday would abruptly stand from the table. She'd glance at Cosa before leaving the room and knew it would follow her shortly.

It would find her, no matter where she had gone, and its greedy fingers would seek their home between her legs. Sometimes, she had enough time to slip off her dress and get comfortable in bed. Other times Cosa would crawl up her leg and slip into her with her dress hiding it from prying eyes and make her come as she stood.

Tonight, Cosa must have sensed she had a lot on her

mind. It slipped a third finger inside, stretching her wide. The sounds of Sunday's arousal filled the room, and she moaned as Cosa picked up the pace and rapidly fucked her. It hooked its middle finger, hitting the special spot deep inside, and pressed its thumb on her swollen clit. Her legs were shaking, and Cosa knew she was close. Its movement stilled as it shoved itself deep inside, thoroughly filling her. That middle finger flicked, and its thumb grinded Sunday into an intense orgasm.

Cosa waited for the shock waves to subside before pulling itself out of her, and she immediately felt empty, missing the way it made her feel full. But sleep threatened her mind, and she hoped as she closed her eyes that her sleep was restful tonight.

TWO

AUGUST

August double-checked that he had everything before he slammed the trunk of his red SUV closed. Weekend bag? Check. Case of craft beer? Check. Cooler of snacks? Check.

This afternoon, Auggie was headed out for his annual guys' trip to Lake Mellow. It was a trip he and four of his closest friends started six years ago when they'd graduated high school. They wanted a trip to cap off their time together at primary school, and they'd kept it up even after they'd graduated from university. Each of them had known that life was about to change for all of them. Each of them had their unique paths set out for them. Well, each of them, except for Auggie.

Luke had his fellowship placement by that point; Andy was about to propose to his high school sweetheart; Evan was studying for the bar; and CJ was already running his software company. Everyone had a path except for Auggie.

That wasn't to say that Auggie hadn't been doing anything since he'd graduated, but nothing that stuck. He'd tried working in the restaurant industry, thinking that maybe he'd open his own place, but it turns out he didn't like working with people that much. Then he thought perhaps it was adults that were the problem, so he got his teaching certificate and taught a whole year at a middle school before deciding that he hated kids.

Now, Auggie was working a monotonous data entry job where he could work from home and not talk to a soul. It was nice until he, you know, wanted to interact with another human being. His friend, CJ, didn't fully understand Auggie's lack of life plan. He was currently sending him job applications for everything from marketing to finance jobs. Even CJ had no idea what Auggie should do.

Auggie was hoping this trip would bring him some much-needed clarity. He was crossing his fingers for something big, loud, and obvious that would tell him what he should do. With how lost he felt, it would need to practically come out and hit him for Auggie to notice it.

Auggie sent a text to the guys' group chat that he was on his way and started the drive. Just three hours stood between him and a relaxing weekend. The guys rented out the same cabin yearly, so Auggie knew how the long weekend would play out. There would be cannonballs into the lake, late-night pool tournaments, maybe a bit of poker, lots of beer, and good grilled food.

These guys were Auggie's rocks. They'd all grown up together in their small town of Wellsford and had been there for each other through everything. They'd seen each other through parents' divorces, deaths of grandparents and beloved pets, braces and growth spurts, girlfriends, and college. They would be there for each other through much more.

The toll road stop beeped as Auggie sped through the passing lane, and he smiled because that meant he only had one hour left in his drive. His exit was coming up soon. From there, it was windy roads through some small town, and on the other side was Lake Mellow. The sun was dipping behind the clouds as Auggie's car veered off the highway and down the off-ramp of Exit 16.

Auggie didn't love this next part of his journey. The town was so small he was convinced that he'd drive through it one year and everything would be abandoned. The town itself sat deep in a valley, so the hills surrounding it stood out. On one of those hills sat a massive old mansion that looked like it was out of the set of a haunted movie. And as Auggie drove through the town, it always looked like the house shifted to watch him.

He kept his eyes on the road as the gravel crunched beneath his tires. Auggie needed something other than the true crime podcast he had been listening to. It certainly wasn't helping the creep factor to hear the gravelly voice describe the details of unsolved missing and murder cases through his car speaker. The ominous traits of the creepy cases being unpacked rang a little too real for Auggie's current surroundings.

No, to get through this part of the drive, Auggie needs

something more upbeat. He picked up his phone from the middle console and swiped through his playlists to find something new. Perhaps the Alt playlist that the guys had put together for their lake trip. There was nothing a little Alabama Shakes couldn't get you through.

Auggie had made this drive plenty of times before, so he was very familiar with the bends of every road and the stop signs that stayed hidden behind overgrown trees. So, he was surprised when he looked up from his phone to see that it looked like a fully grown Holly tree had been transplanted into the middle of a bend. He'd noticed this tree before, but it'd always been further up the hill. It looked like someone had picked it up and plopped it right down in the gravel, blocking the path of any cars.

He slammed on his brakes and squinted his eyes tight, fear gripping his chest, but his tires spun on the gravel before they could catch, and Auggie slammed right into the bark of that Holly tree.

A ringing in his ears and the clicking of his hazards brought Auggie back to the present. He looked around his car at the mess the crash had made. His airbag had deployed, leaving a chalky substance over his dashboard and lap. The case of beer had shattered, and his entire car smelled like the inside of a brewery. But Auggie was okay, at least as far as he could tell.

He groaned as he pushed open the driver's door and caught himself before falling onto the dusty road. *Fuck.* He reached back into the car to search for his phone, his fingers grazing shards of glass as he riffled through the debris of broken windows. He wiped the airbag dust off his hands and looked around. Where was he?

The sun was almost fully set now, so he needed to figure out somewhere to go and fast. Auggie tried to pry open the back doors, thinking maybe his phone had slipped through the seat, but the metal was bent and dented too much to function. He could see smoke billowing out of his hood, so he knew he wouldn't be able to keep driving tonight. His best bet was to find somewhere with a phone so he could call the guys, and maybe one of them would come get him, and he could tow his car somewhere.

Auggie spun around to try and see how far the main part of town might be from here. He could walk there but wasn't confident anything would be open. When he turned around, he noticed the house. When he drove through town, the house felt so far away. Like it sat high on a hill that would always be out of your reach, but now it felt closer than ever. Had it always been this close to the road?

He didn't like the idea of walking up to that house, but at this point, he didn't have any other options. Auggie dug his feet into the dirt and made his way up the hill. The house seemed to double in size the closer Auggie got, and a large iron fence stood around the massive plot of land it sat on. He walked up to the gates and pushed a button on the metal intercom box sticking out of the ground.

Static buzzed before a quiet male answered from the other side, "Strange residence."

"Uh, hi, I—" Auggie looked around, feeling silly talking

into this metal box, "I wrecked my car down the hill. I was wondering if I could use your phone?"

No one responded, but the large metal gates swung open. Auggie took that as a sign to go ahead and walk in. Inside the gates were tall evergreens, rows of rose bushes, and neatly trimmed hedges. His feet crunched on pea gravel as he made his way up to the circle drive in front of the mansion. Turrets jutted out from the sides, and stained-glass windows filled one entire corner. Smooth stone and marble gargoyle statues flanked the corners of the roof, and Auggie almost tripped on the steps as he stared at the expanse of the home. *What kind of people live here?*

Before he could even knock, one of the double doors pulled open, letting the glow of the interior lights leak out onto the front steps. A man, who must be a butler based on his crisp black and white suit, stood on the other side. A woman dressed in all black, with long, straight black hair, rushed to the door.

"Oh, dear! Are you okay? I heard the crash from all the way up here." The woman's eyes were filled with worry, her porcelain skin almost glowing in the light.

Auggie turned back around to gesture to his car down the hill and furrowed his brows in confusion. What felt like a short distance a little bit ago now felt like a world away. He couldn't even see the tree that he ran into from here. *That's odd.*

"Yeah, I think so." Auggie shook his head as he faced the woman again. "I really need to use your phone to call some friends. I'm sorry to bother you. I didn't know how far the main part of town would be."

The woman gestured to him to come inside. "It's not a bother, dear. I'm Tish; this is Magnus, don't mind him." Auggie nodded at the butler, who stayed quiet. "Come on inside, dear. It's getting chilly out there."

"Thank you, I'm August." Auggie stepped inside and was surprised to find the house warm and comforting despite its ominous look from the outside. Cobwebs lined the corners of the entry, but in a way that felt intentional, like they were giving a home to spiders.

"Would you like some tea?" Tish asked Auggie as he tried not to gape at the inside of this house. It's beautiful in a weird, vintage, almost haunted way. There were flickering candles on nearly every surface, beautiful wooden furniture, and plush antique rugs over glossy hardwood floors. Oddities sat behind glass domes scattered across tabletops. A tiny skull here, a glob of liquid with something floating in it over there.

"Um, sure," Auggie answered as he followed the woman, hoping there was a phone in the room she was going to make the tea in.

Auggie followed her into a large kitchen that almost felt more industrial than homey. A large chunk of green and black marble sat in the middle of the room on top of wooden legs. Copper pots and pans sat displayed on open shelves against the wall. Tish went over to a deep, worn copper sink to fill a kettle with water.

She lit the gas stove to heat the water and brought down two teacups from a cupboard. He didn't want to rush her, but Auggie really needed a phone. At this point, he wasn't even sure this house *had* phone service.

"The curve down the hill really has a way of sneaking up on people," Tish said with her back to him as she prepped the teacups with sugar.

"Yeah, it really does. It kind of felt like it came out of nowhere. I didn't notice it was that far down the hill last year." Auggie was still perplexed at that. He'd made this drive in the pitch of the night before, having had to wait until his shift at the restaurant was over before he could make the trip last year. He'd seen the tree up on the hill and appreciated its size from the road. Maybe this area had seen lots of rain this year and eroded some of that hill away.

Tish turned to him with a smile on her face that wasn't quite comforting, "That's certainly odd." She poured hot water into our cups, added a tea bag, and slid it over.

"But if I could just use a phone, I can call someone to come get me so I can get out of your way," Auggie mentioned it again as another reminder in case she forgot. She didn't seem to have any urgency in getting him to a phone.

"Of course, dear, let me grab it for you," the woman answered and turned, leaving Auggie in the kitchen alone. He glanced around, curiously eyeing a pot on the stove that's nearly bubbling over with something green.

Well, he thought he was alone. As he glanced around the room, he nearly dropped his mug as he caught the eyes of a girl standing in the back doorway. She was dressed in a tight black dress, creamy skin smooth in the dim light. Her dark black hair was in tight braids on either side of her face, and her wide, black eyes stared at him.

They locked eyes, so he couldn't ignore her. He said, "Hey."

"Is your car okay?" She ignored his hello but stepped through the doorway and into the light of the kitchen. She was beautiful in a quiet, subdued way. Her lips were full and rosy, her cheeks flushed like she had come back from a run.

"Uh, no, not really. I think it's totaled." Auggie's brain stuttered a bit as he took her in like he was convinced he'd met her before, but he knew he hadn't.

"Where were you headed?" the girl asked.

"Lake Mellow." Auggie took a sip of the tea, its heat warming his throat. "For a guys' trip."

"I'm sorry that you'll miss it," she said.

"Well, actually, I just need a phone so I can—"

"Ah, Sunday, dear, we have a guest!" Tish came back into the kitchen, noticeably without a phone. "August, dear, follow me. The phone is this way."

Auggie didn't know why Tish had kept him waiting, but he shook any nefarious thoughts out of his head as he slid off his stool to follow the woman through the doorway. Auggie knew he listened to too many true crime podcasts for his own good, so he kept the creeping thoughts shoved in the back of his mind.

He passed by the girl, Sunday, on his way out of the kitchen, and a tingly feeling zapped in his belly. This house was weird. This family was weird.

Tish led him to a small office off the main foyer. High

shelves were stacked to the brim with books, journals, and loose sheets of paper. Small trinkets littered the shelves, and Auggie looked curiously at the items tucked behind glass boxes. Skulls of small animals, feathers, and odd jars of liquid were on display. The woman pointed to an old black phone on a side table, and Auggie had to stop himself from rushing toward it, hoping it would have a dial tone.

Auggie had the receiver off the hook, a dial tone, in fact, ringing in his ear, ready to punch in the first number when he realized he didn't know any of his friends' numbers by heart. In fact, the only number he could recall on command was his old house number, which now didn't exist because his parents had gotten rid of their landline last year.

Auggie slumped in the leather chair next to the table and hung up the phone.

"Is there a problem?" It was the girl, Sunday. She was standing in the doorway of the study, staring at Auggie.

"Yeah, I—I don't actually know a number to call. I guess I hit that tree harder than I thought." Auggie chuckled, because what else can you do in a moment like this, and ran his hands over his face.

"That's unfortunate." Sunday's voice was blunt and deadpan when she spoke.

"I'll need to go back down to my car and find my phone. If I have it, I can call someone." Auggie stood up and wiped his hands on his jeans with determination now that he had a plan.

A loud crack of thunder and a flash of lightning that

filled the room killed his motivation. Tish appeared back in the doorway and peered at Sunday, then at Auggie.

"Do you need to stay here tonight, dear? That's quite the storm that's starting out there." Auggie was glad Tish offered before he had to ask. He hated imposing on other people. He was already dreading having to call his friends to ask them to drive an hour to come get him. This way, he could call a tow truck in the morning and maybe rent a vehicle to make the rest of the drive himself. He wished he could text them to update them on his status so they wouldn't worry.

An idea sparked in Auggie's mind, "Hey, do you happen to have any internet here?" Auggie was hopeful because if he could log in to his social media, he could try to message one of his friends to let them know what happened.

Tish and Sunday looked at each other, and before they could speak, another clap of thunder rattled the house, and the entire room was bathed in darkness.

THREE

SUNDAY

The vision had jolted through Sunday's body so viciously that she fell to her knees in the hallway outside her bedroom. Somehow, she knew that this vision wasn't something that *had* happened in the past or something that was *about* to happen in the future. No, this time, the vision was something that was happening in real time.

Sunday could hear the red SUV screech its brakes moments before the driver realized they were about to slam into a tree. She heard the crunch of metal, the same sound she'd been plagued with for months, as it bent around the trunk of the Holly tree at the base of their property. She could feel the fear of the driver as they squeezed their eyes tight on impact, and she felt the breath leave their chest as the airbag deployed, knocking the wind out of them.

The driver took shape as a young man in her vision as he climbed out of the vehicle and looked around, and something deep in her belly zapped when his eyes settled on her home. She had stood in the darkness of the foyer when Magnus, their butler, and her mother answered the door. Her breath had quickened when she first heard his name, August.

August.

Sunday tested the name of the man on her lips. Finally, there was a name to the face and face to the feeling of someone she'd been given through her visions. But why?

Sunday's visions had always been about people unrelated to her existence. They were always dead or dying or hoping for death. But this man was alive and well, albeit disheveled, and in her home. So, when he sat alone in her kitchen, she knew she had to see him.

He had spotted her. His eyes had immediately found hers as if they were destined to, and he'd almost dropped the teacup her mother had given him. Sunday had followed him to the study as he anxiously sought their home phone to call someone for help, and she couldn't name the feeling that flooded her belly when he realized he didn't know who to call.

She was ready to offer to help him look for his phone in the wreckage of his car to hold on to the feeling for a bit longer when the thunder had cracked outside, and rain poured down. And now he was here. Staying the night in her home. Mother had set him up in a guest room, which sat a few doors down from Sunday's.

She didn't know what to do now.

There was so much pent-up energy in her belly from

seeing one of her visions in flesh and blood and in her *home*. There was another unknown feeling bubbling deep inside.

August.

Sunday whispered the name to herself again as she crept down the carpeted hallway to her bedroom. She needed to release this newfound tension.

She shut the door to her bedroom behind her. Her chest heaved like she was out of breath, but she didn't know what from. Cosa was already here, and Sunday knew exactly what would help her feel better. She reached for the hem of her dress and tugged it over her head, walking toward her bathroom.

Sunday turned the knob of her shower to the hottest it would go, lit a few extra candles around her bathroom to light her way since the power was out, and dug around her nightstand drawer for something to take the edge off. She pulled out a dark purple vibrator, thick and ribbed—she needed the big guns out tonight.

You could probably say that Cosa had turned Sunday into a bit of an addict. At the slightest bout of tension, she would seek release in the form of an orgasm. What used to be only her fingers turned into toys as she got older, and with the aid of Cosa, had turned into much, much more. Sunday was the kind of girl who needed to find her release often, sometimes multiple times a day. With a quiet mansion and a reclusive life, it was easy to live this way.

Sunday opened her shower door, the steam already fogging up the bathroom, and stepped inside, hissing as the hot water touched her skin. She kept the door open for Cosa as it entered behind her and stood, waiting for her on the small bench at the end of the shower. Sunday let the hot water ease the tension in her shoulders first. She reached to undo her braids and let the water soak up her hair, the black tendrils curling over her cheeks.

As her eyes were closed under the stream of water, she felt Cosa massage soap into her skin, and she sighed at its touch. Its slippery fingers worked knots out of her shoulders and slid down her spine to massage her backside. She felt the soap slip in between her cheeks, and goosebumps pricked her skin as Cosa trailed further down still.

Cosa used its fingers to warm up her middle, and she swayed slightly as it dipped one of those fingers deep inside her. Sunday leaned forward to grab her toy and reached down to hand it to Cosa. It took it in an instant and slid it through her wet folds. She widened her stance a bit, braced one hand on the tiled wall, and let out a deep breath.

Cosa teased her entrance with the toy, just barely sliding it in before pulling it back out. Her breath was heavy, and a moan escaped her throat as it finally pressed the device past her entrance and settled it deep inside. She knew as soon as Cosa turned it on, she wouldn't last long. As she closed her eyes, Sunday didn't see blackness as she usually did. Instead, this time, she pictured the face of the stranger settling in down the hall.

August.

Cosa pressed the button on, found her favorite setting, and pressed the toy in and out slowly. Sunday felt the ribs of the toy flex and buzz against her insides, and her arousal pooled in between her legs. She gasped as Cosa pressed the button again, increasing the intensity of the vibrations.

She didn't hold back her moan as she exploded, her body shaking violently as liquid dripped out onto Cosa. Behind her eyelids, Sunday kept picturing August.

There were no chirping birds to wake Sunday at 1313 Hallow Lane. Instead, she typically woke from the smell of coffee Cosa would bring her or a vision. This morning was no different, and as the sun was rising from the other side of the hill, she sat straight up, jolting awake from a vision, as she saw August make his way past her bedroom and downstairs.

She quickly put her hair in braids, slid on another black dress, the one she had taken off last night already put away in the hamper, and made her way downstairs. She found August at her kitchen counter, hands gripping a mug of hot coffee. Sunday was rather fond of hands. An obsession only made stronger with Cosa and its skills. So, she eyed August's hands in appraisal. His hands were wide, with prominent veins across the back and long, thick fingers. She approved.

Her father was annoyingly cheerful this morning, chatting with August about the wild storm that had raged last night. The power had just come back on, and she could tell August was too kind to interrupt her father. But she knew he was ready to leave, move on, and forget about his night in this odd place. She knew it because she could feel it.

Sunday didn't want August to leave, but she didn't know

why. She never wanted strangers around. As she was about to turn to leave the kitchen and go find Cousin Itta, he turned to her. His eyes were brighter today, a warm honey brown as opposed to her inky black ones. Sunday didn't notice eyes, at least not on living people. She was currently in the middle of learning how to identify a clearer window to establish a time of death depending on the hemorrhaging inside a corpse's eyeball.

"Good morning," August said, and something hammered in her chest.

"It is another dreadful day, yes," Sunday muttered back as she walked into the kitchen. She might as well get some coffee now that he'd spotted her.

August chuckled at her comment like she wasn't serious and tipped his mug back, draining it. "Well, tell your wife I appreciate her letting me stay last night," he said to my father. "I'm going to head down to get my phone so I can call for some assistance."

Her mother would still be sleeping. On storms like last night, Mother and Itta would use the energy to summon up conversations with their ancestors into the early morning hours. They probably wouldn't see either of them until dinner.

"I can help you look." The words were out of Sunday's mouth before she could stop them and based on the raised eyebrows of both men in the room and the grunt from Magnus out in the foyer, everyone was as surprised as she was.

"Sure, yeah, that would be really helpful." August

grinned at her, and for once in her life, she didn't roll her eyes at a smile. Sunday simply turned on her heel and headed out the front door, knowing that August would follow.

"So do you go to school around here . . . or?" August was trying to make small talk with Sunday as they made their way down the hill from her house. The sun had crested over the hill, and the air around them was thick with summer heat. *Dreadful.*

"I take online classes," Sunday answered.

"Cool. What are you studying?" This is why Sunday avoided strangers. Typically, she would turn on her heel and walk away from nonessential discourse. She did it all the time. But her feet wouldn't let her move. Instead, they betrayed her and kept taking steps down the hill.

"Forensics," she answered.

"Oh, wow, that's so cool!" And August did look like he thought it was cool. His face didn't hold the usual odd brow furrow that the people in town had when they looked at Sunday or her family. He was probably just really good at being polite.

"I graduated with a degree in business," August continued the conversation as if Sunday asked. She didn't, but she was curious. "And it has served me, zero." He held his hand up and made an "o" with his fingers pressed against his thumb.

"That's unfortunate," Sunday said.

August chuckled, but not mockingly like other people have done, more like in a way that showed her odd answers intrigued him.

"This walk down here is a lot further than the walk up last night was," August commented out loud.

"Time and space have a way of shaping themselves differently in stress," she said.

"Mmm, yeah, I guess you're right," August agreed, and if Sunday knew how to smile, she would've.

They made it to the car, and the scene looked gruesome in the light of day, so much so that August flinched when he saw his SUV. His hands grazed over the smashed hood, and his shoes crunched over broken glass. He took in the scene, and Sunday did the same.

It was hard for her to reconcile the scene before her since she'd already seen bits and pieces of it in her mind for months. The real-life images shifted and clicked together with images from her vision, forming a complete picture.

August pried open the driver's side door and carefully reached in to search for his phone. With an impact as great as this one was, who knew where the phone was at this point. Sunday walked to the passenger side, opened the door, and started helping him look.

Suddenly, a buzz echoed through the car, and both August and Sunday flinched at the sound. The noise was coming from underneath the seat. It was his phone. Someone was calling him.

Sunday felt a weird pang in her gut at the hopeful look on his face. They both moved to the backseat, the sound coming from underneath a seat somewhere. They tried to jerk open the back doors, but the metal wouldn't budge, so instead they both climbed into the backseat over the middle console.

She slid across the back seat to look when she felt a sharp sting on her palm. Slowly raising her hand up, Sunday saw blood bead up to the surface of her palm and drip down her wrist.

"Shit! You're hurt, uh . . ." August stopped looking for the phone and started frantically looking for something to wrap her hand with, and as he did, Sunday stared, mesmerized by the way the red liquid crisscrossed down her arm.

August tugged his duffle bag out of the back and dug around to find a shirt. He ripped a section off, tearing the hem with his teeth, and came to stand on Sunday's side to wrap her hand. He was breathing heavily, and she could smell the mint body wash her parents kept in the guestroom shower.

August was naked in her house last night. Perhaps at the same time, she was naked in her shower. She didn't know why that thought mattered to her. August was what Sunday and Itta called a "normie." Normies were off limits for the Strange family, not because they were deemed unworthy, but because they were usually unsafe.

The Strange family was aware they were their own unique breed of weird. And that was fine with them. They had generations of familial history of going against the grain, believing (and using) magic, summoning ghosts, seeing visions, sleeping in coffins, and collecting weird occult artifacts. *They* were okay with their weirdness.

But most other people weren't. And if that person was a

normie, someone who didn't have the same odd proclivities as the Strange family did, then that person might not be safe. In the age of judging first, asking questions later, Sunday couldn't risk mingling with a normie.

Not that she knew how to mingle at all.

August held her palm tight and high above her head to keep the blood flowing down. His phone continued to buzz behind her. Sunday knew that he wanted to find it. Answer it. Call for help. But instead, he stood and held her bleeding hand.

"I think I'm fine now," she said, "I can hold my own hand up."

August smiled down at her, his stupid grin lopsided and his warm eyes sparkling. He slowly let go of her hand as if he was testing her word. His eyes traced the lines of dried blood heading up her forearm and past her elbow like he was assessing her coherence.

Finally, he nodded and headed to the other side of the car to continue his search for his phone. It only took a minute for him to spot it buzzing again deep underneath the driver's side seat. He held onto the door with one hand and patted his hand on the floorboard with the other.

Sunday noted how his arm and shoulder muscles shifted as he moved.

She heard him grunt as he finally made contact with the device, and he let out a breath as he gripped his still buzzing phone in his hand. His eyes scanned the screen, and he swiped at the phone to answer it.

"Hello," August answered out of breath. "Luke, it's Auggie—hello?"

August goes by Auggie.

Auggie.

Sunday tested the shortened version of his name on her tongue.

Auggie.

He pulled his phone away from his ear in confusion. He tapped at the screen, "Shit. It's dead."

"That's unfortunate," she said.

Auggie threw his head back in laughter, "Yeah, Sunday, it is rather unfortunate."

This was the first time she'd heard him speak her name. It stirred the same odd feeling that had been lingering in her gut all morning. She didn't hate it.

"Do you have a charger?" Sunday asked, "You could charge it back at the house."

And for the second time in less than twenty-four hours, another member of the Strange family invited a stranger into their home.

FOUR

AUGUST

There was definitely something wrong with the wiring in this house, Auggie thought as he tried yet another outlet to charge his phone. He had been so close to the outside world. He had held his vibrating phone in his hand as Luke was calling, and yet it had died right after he swiped to answer it.

Auggie had been distracted by Sunday. She'd cut her hand on a shard of window glass in the back seat of his car, and the sight of her blood had caused his heart to beat out of his chest. She had sat on the edge of the back seat, arm raised, eyes locked on her own blood as it trailed down her arm, and Auggie had sprung into action.

He still remembered the softness of her skin as he held her arm above her head and the way her pitch-black eyes had held his as he caught his breath. There was something about this girl that made Auggie curious. Her deadpan humor, morbid fascinations, and wide eyes captivated him.

There had to be a lot more to Sunday Strange, and he wished he could get to know it all. He didn't miss the way her eyes tracked him as he walked around her home or the front garden. Auggie got the impression that she was just as curious about him.

He released a frustrated sigh as he watched his phone light up, but it never actually turned on. Maybe something about that storm last night zapped the electrical lines, making them only half work. He glanced up from his spot on the floor of the home office to see Sunday.

She had this way of knowing exactly where he was always. He wasn't sure how she did it, considering how massive this house was. Auggie hadn't taken a full tour, but on his hunt for different outlets this morning, he'd come across a home library, a theater room, multiple guest bedrooms, and a small conservatory. One thing was for sure: the Strange family were loaded.

"There's something still wrong with the power. Or maybe the storm zapped my phone or something," Auggie said to Sunday.

She nodded but didn't say anything. He was expecting one of her deadpan *"that's unfortunate"* statements that made him laugh for no reason.

"I think I'll walk down into town to try and charge it there," Auggie said as he got up off the floor.

"I'll go with you," Sunday said as she made her way toward the front door. Auggie was hoping she would offer.

On the way out, they passed by the dining room where Sunday's family was seated for breakfast. It was an odd bunch, that's for sure. The house was made up of what looked like multi-generations. There were grandparents, perhaps an uncle and cousin, Sunday's parents, and, of course, their quiet butler.

Auggie swore he saw a detached hand scurry across the top of the table, but obviously, his mind was playing tricks on him. He shook his head to clear it and followed her out the front door. The summer sun was in full force, and it wasn't even noon yet. Auggie wished he was lying on the dock at the cabin with the guys.

"We have a dock here over behind the house. There's a swamp that borders the property," Sunday said as they made their way back down the hill. Did she know he was thinking of the dock at Lake Mellow?

"That's cool. Your property is massive. Have you always lived here?" Auggie wanted to get to know Sunday, and what better way to do that than to pepper her with questions as they made the long walk into town.

"Yes, it's been in my family for hundreds of years. I've lived here my whole life." Auggie noticed she could have answered him with one word, but she gave him more this time.

"It's certainly unique, I can see why you wouldn't want to leave," Auggie said, and he could feel Sunday's eyes on him.

"The developers in the lake town have tried for years to get us to sell. They want to build an outlet mall on our property," Sunday said with venom on her tongue.

"Don't let them." Auggie turned to face her, and she nodded in response.

They finally made their way down the hill and were on the flat expanse of the road. Auggie turned back to look at the house and was still in disbelief at how far away it seemed by the light of day. He must have been in shock last night when he walked up here. He could've sworn it only took him a minute, but both trips down today have taken at least fifteen.

"So, what do you plan on doing in forensics?" Auggie asked, desperate for Sunday to speak more. Her voice was soft and gentle, but coupled with the bluntness she added, it made him smile.

"I want to help the police with more unsolved cases. I've been able to help detectives with a few already. It'd be nice to do more of that," Sunday answered.

"Wow, that's pretty incredible." Auggie didn't hide his surprise and awe because, of course, this girl did something huge like solving old crime cases. He thought back to that unsolved case he was listening to last night right before he was going to switch it over to his playlist. Could Sunday help someone like them?

"I guess." Sunday simply shrugged at his compliment.

"Do you ever, I don't know, like, leave this place, or . . .?" Auggie let his question trail off because he didn't know what he was trying to ask.

"Why would I? If I leave, I have to deal with people," Sunday answered matter-of-factly.

Auggie chuckled. "Yeah, that is true. And people, well, they kind of suck, don't they?"

Auggie heard the bass of the music coming from the truck before he saw it. Without thinking, he tugged at Sunday's arm and pulled her closer to him off the gravel of the road. As the truck barreled by, kicking dust up behind it, he felt her press into his side and grip his t-shirt.

He could feel her breasts pressed up against his arm and the warmth of her body. He looked down at where she had his t-shirt gripped, and Sunday looked up at him with wide eyes. Auggie would love to see those eyes looking up at him from somewhere else.

God, it's been a while since he'd gotten laid. Even longer since someone had given him a blow job; he must be desperate if he was getting a chubby in ninety-degree heat while walking into a creepy ghost town with a girl he only met yesterday.

Get it together, August.

Sunday licked her bottom lip and released the grip on his shirt. Auggie wondered what she tasted like. He wondered if she would like it if he tugged on those braids as he fucked her. He wondered if she wore anything underneath these black dresses or if she would be waiting bare for him.

Auggie cleared his throat and turned from Sunday, hoping she wouldn't notice the bulge in his pants. They kept walking, but she stayed closer to his side than she was earlier, sometimes bumping up against his arm as they walked. Auggie had to think about baseball and sauerkraut to get his dick to cooperate.

They walked quietly for another few minutes, each of them lost in their own thoughts. He could only hope that Sunday's were as dirty as his were. Before long, they'd made it to the main street of town.

Auggie wasn't too far off in thinking it was a ghost town. There was a small grocery store, a pharmacy, and a liquor store open. But between those were other small shops that had definitely seen better days. Dust caked the large windows of nearly every shop, and newspapers lined some of the panes to hide what was behind the glass.

He decided to try out the grocery store to see if he could buy a battery pack or a new charger for his phone. The clerk, an acne-riddled teenage boy, let him plug his phone into an outlet on the back counter, and Auggie left it there while he looked around the store.

This store hadn't been updated in decades. Even the packaging of the food looked like it was from the '80s. Auggie and Sunday got a few hard and curious stares from other shoppers as they made their way down the aisles. This made Auggie stare a few down and pull her closer to him.

By the time they found the measly electronics section, Auggie had his hand on her lower back. She didn't flinch, nor did she move away, so Auggie kept it there, making small circles on her tailbone with his finger. He picked up a new charging cord and backup power bank and headed to the register.

The teenager didn't even look up at them as he rang him up. Auggie and Sunday made their way back over the counter where Auggie's phone waited, its screen lit brightly. *Success.*

As they stood there waiting for the phone to fully power on, Auggie heard whispers and giggles from behind them.

He turned and saw a group of girls, probably around Sunday's age, huddled together in an aisle, staring at them, and whispering to each other. Sunday didn't look over, but Auggie could tell she was aware of them, too. He noticed the way her back straightened and her jaw clenched. Her eyes unfocused as she tried to pay attention to anywhere else but there.

And so, he decided to give the town gossip something to actually report on. Auggie dropped his phone on the counter and turned toward Sunday. He threaded his fingers through her hand, bringing her knuckles up to his mouth, and placing a gentle kiss there. Auggie didn't look away from her face as he pulled her body close to his and slid his arm around her waist. He leaned his cheek against hers as he picked his phone back up to see if it had powered on.

He thought he saw the subtlest of grins twitch in the corner of her mouth. Auggie's phone was working again, and with Sunday at his hip, he swiped through to the group chat to update the guys.

Auggie frowned as he saw exactly zero messages waiting for him there. Not a single text from one of the guys asking where he was. He told them he was heading out. In fact, CJ had even sent back a GIF. Auggie could see it right here. He checked for voicemails. *Nothing.* He checked for messages on his social media profiles. *Nothing.*

Auggie chalked it up to poor cell service and sent his own update to the group thread.

Got stuck in Mellow Township, and the car was totaled. I'm trying to get it towed today, anyone down to come pick me up?

Auggie decided to go ahead and give Luke a call back since he had been the one to reach out this morning. The line rang in Auggie's ear, but no one picked up. Auggie left a voicemail but wasn't confident Luke had ever set it up. After rechecking his texts again, and still finding no response, Auggie locked his screen so it could keep charging.

He looked down at Sunday, her black eyes threatening to swallow him whole, and he shrugged, "Is there a body shop around here?"

Sunday turned to head back out on the street, so Auggie tucked his phone away under a stack of papers so it could keep charging while they were out. He jogged to catch up with her, and his hand found its spot on her shoulder, almost subconsciously. When he did, she let him tug her close to his chest; he was half afraid she'd take two steps away from him. Something about Sunday eased Auggie's anxiety so he was glad she was sticking close.

Sunday led him around the block where there was a gas station and a car repair shop that were, miraculously, occupied. Auggie loosened his hold on her shoulder but brought his hand down to grip hers as they walked up to the old man working underneath a hood, and again, she let him.

"Excuse me?" Auggie hollered as they got closer to the man. The man lifted up from the engine, his eyes on them curiously.

"Do you offer tow services? I wrecked my car up Hallow

Lane last night, and I think it's totaled." Auggie pointed behind him toward the hill, but the man kept the odd look on his face.

"Can I help you?" the old man asked accusingly.

This time, Sunday spoke up, "Can we get a tow? His car is wrecked on Hallow Lane."

The old man's eyes flicked between Sunday and Auggie. "Yeah. Won't be able to get to it till this afternoon, though. We only got the one truck, and Harold's out with it right now," the man answered.

"That's okay. You don't happen to offer rental cars, do you?" Auggie asked, even though he would've bet money on the answer being no.

The man stared back at them, clearly uncomfortable they were still there, "Rental. Cars. Do. You. Have. One." Sunday enunciated each word.

The man chuckled and shook his head. "No, girl, no rental cars here. Your best bet is to have someone you know," he wiped his forehead with a grease-stained rag, "drive ya to where ya need to be."

"Alright, well, thank you. My car is the red SUV wrapped around that old Holly tree up the road. You can't miss it." Auggie walked away as the man hollered his promise to get it off the road before dark. Not that it mattered to Auggie. The car was useless to him now.

Auggie and Sunday made their way back to the grocery store, where Auggie purchased a large Gatorade and bag of Cheetos. He was pretty sure the Strange family home didn't have snacks like this. He picked his phone off the charger when it had about 32 percent battery life. He hoped it was enough to last him until he got ahold of one of the guys.

Auggie was disappointed to see that no one had messaged him back, and his call to Luke still went unanswered. Auggie tried each of the other guys and got the same response. This area must be in a dead zone, he didn't want to think how far he'd have to walk in ninety-plus degree heat to find a spot where he'd catch a good signal.

At this point his only hope was to cross his fingers that Luke would call back, and that Auggie would be able to answer it in time for it to connect. For now, he was ready to get back to the coolness of Sunday's house and get out of this dusty valley.

The feel of Auggie's hand in Sunday's was warm. It wasn't sweaty like you might think with how hot the sun was beating down. It wasn't clammy or suffocating like she had assumed it might feel. Instead, it just felt *right*.

When Auggie pulled her in tight and kissed her knuckles, her knees nearly gave out from underneath her. She had wanted to drag his face down to hers and see what his lips felt like. She wanted to run her fingers through the brown curls that set on top of his head and scratch her palms down his cheeks that needed shaving.

She had barely noticed the girls who were snickering in the middle of the bread aisle. Sunday had long ago learned to drown out the whispers and weighted glances that strangers always gave when her family came to town. There was no reason for them to come down the hill anymore. Her father now had everything delivered straight to the house. The pick-ings in town were too slim.

But Sunday realized she didn't hate the visit to the town as much as she normally did with Auggie there. With his hand on her lower back, arm thrown over her shoulder, or palm in hers, she didn't mind it. But she also knew that if he kept looking at her the way he did and kept thinking about her how he was, then Sunday wouldn't be able to help herself for much longer.

As they had made their walk into town, she saw tiny scraps of a vision. It was so detailed, but not one that she had come up with on her own. She realized, after noticing Auggie adjust the bulge in his jeans, that she was getting glimpses of what *his* mind was thinking.

And his mind was dirty. Sunday saw her head thrown back as he gripped her braids tightly and pounded into her from behind. She saw her own eyes wide with tears in the corners as Auggie shoved his dick in her open mouth. She glimpsed Auggie shooting streams of his warm orgasm over her belly.

Sunday had to focus on anything else to keep the visions at bay. They were tormenting her because she desperately wanted to see them come to life. If she knew they both wanted each other, how much longer did they need to wait to make it happen?

As soon as they had gotten back to the house, Sunday had left Auggie in the foyer as she went to her room, feeling confused about all the emotions swirling in her belly. She didn't even need to wait for Cosa as she leaned against her locked bedroom door, slid her hand up her dress, and brought on her own release with just her fingers.

She lay down after that, but before long, she sat up in bed as another vision jolted her awake. This time it wasn't visions of blow jobs and fucking Auggie. No, this was a vision much like the one she'd gotten almost two weeks ago that she'd yet to tell anyone about.

She didn't know *how* she knew, but Sunday was certain these visions were about her future. And they were years from now, decades even. And, yet she looked exactly the same. She lived in this home as the lady of the house. She'd get glimpses of Itta and Cosa, and she smiled, knowing she'd have some familiar faces in her eternal life.

But the thing that made Sunday gasp for air was the glimpse of someone new. In the vision of her immortality was a now familiar head of brown curls, honey-brown eyes, and veiny hands. In Sunday's eternal life was Auggie.

Sunday needed to speak with someone about her new visions. Maybe her mother or Itta would know how to decipher them. Maybe they weren't even true, but perhaps what she *wanted* to see.

She got up and set out to find Itta.

Luckily, Itta and Mother were having tea together in the conservatory. Now, she only had to tell this story once. They both went quiet when Sunday approached, as if they knew she would join them and had news.

So, Sunday told them. She told them about the first vision she got nearly two weeks ago and what she thought it meant. She told them about the vision she had and how Auggie had made an appearance.

"What does it mean?" Sunday asked as she finished filling them in.

Itta and Mother glanced at each other before Itta answered, "Well, you've definitely been chosen by our ancestors to live eternally. This is exciting news."

"But what about August?" Sunday didn't want to call him by his nickname in front of them. She wanted to hold on to that for herself.

Mother spoke up, "It is rare for the magic to choose someone so far outside of the family to live an eternal life. But it isn't unheard of."

"The key that you need to understand, Sunday," Itta said, "is that you already know the consequences of living an eternal life. August doesn't." She sat her teacup in the saucer, the ceramic clinking, as she continued, "This means that he'll need to make the choice to stay with you willingly. He cannot be persuaded by magic to stay, nor can he be forced to stay."

Sunday's face was blank as she took in this information.

Itta cleared her throat as she added, "Now that you've acknowledged his potential for immortality, the magic that has been keeping him here will release its hold. Be ready for him to leave, Sunday."

She turned on her heel without another word and left her mother and Itta in the conservatory. That was that. Auggie would have no interest in staying, and she knew there was nothing she could do to convince him otherwise. How would she even start that conversation?

Hey, Auggie, this house is magical, and I come from a line of psychic witches. They call me The Raven because my visions are usually of death, but lately, I've been seeing you and me living in eternal happiness. All you have to do is leave everything you know behind forever.

No, Sunday didn't see that conversation going over well. Apparently, the magic had been working in her favor this entire time. How else would you explain the lack of cell service or internet when her home normally functioned just fine? How else would you explain the fact that he couldn't get through to his friends?

And yet, despite the magic's strength, he was still trying everything he could to get ahold of someone so he could leave. And why wouldn't he? He was a normie trapped in an odd mansion full of strange people and things. Heck, he hadn't even *met* Cosa.

As the magic pulled back, things would start working more in his favor. Auggie would get his messages to go through, or one of his friends would finally answer. It was only a matter of time.

For some reason, the magic continued to stay on her side, and Auggie was still struggling to get service as the afternoon turned into the evening. With the smell of a full-course dinner wafting in from the kitchen, she hoped Auggie would stay. At least for tonight.

Sunday noted Cosa had made itself scarce since Auggie has been here. There's only so much a stranger from the outside world could reconcile with, and a walking hand typically wasn't one of them. So, she was pleasantly surprised to see Cosa waiting for her on top of her desk as she came out of the bathroom to head down for dinner.

Maybe another quick release was what she needed to ease her anxiety about what to do about Auggie. She *wanted* Auggie to stay. She wanted Auggie to do *a lot* of things. Like sneak into her room and destroy her. But he'd have to come to those terms himself. And Sunday didn't have much trust in normies to be confident that would happen.

Sunday slipped her hands underneath her dress and slid off her black lace panties as she watched Cosa. It pulled out her desk chair, silently encouraging her to sit. She hiked up the hem of her dress, so it pooled around her waist and leaned back in the chair.

Cosa hopped down from her desk and landed on her thighs, its walk up them tickling her. It traced small lines on her tender skin with a fingertip, and Sunday leaned her head back and sighed deeply. She gasped as a finger slid down her middle, coating itself in her arousal. Cosa slid a finger in, only to the first knuckle, and she relaxed into its touch.

Cosa added another finger, still not going past her entrance, and Sunday groaned, craving its fullness. It took its cue and shoved two fingers deep inside her, filling her up. Cosa pulled itself in and out of her, her arousal pooling in between her thighs. Her insides pulsed around its fingers, and she gripped them with her muscles.

Sunday pulled her knees up to rest on either side of the chair, and Cosa pressed deep into her, grinding its palm against her clit. She knew she wouldn't last much longer, and when it pressed into her backside with its pinky finger, she came undone. Sunday exploded all over Cosa, her arousal soaking it, and her breath came in gasps. She needed that release.

Cosa pulled out of her, and Sunday sat up, wiped herself off in the bathroom, and walked out of her bedroom to head to dinner. She decided not to put her panties back on.

SIX

Auggie had stepped out of his room when he heard the gasp. He got the feeling that his hallway neighbor, Sunday, was a little horn dog. He knew, now, that her flushed cheeks meant she'd just made herself come.

She thought she was sneaky every time she'd tuck away to head upstairs or behind a dark corner where she would rub herself to orgasm. He'd heard her last night in the shower, and he had wanted so badly to knock on her door after to see if he could join her. He was also in desperate need of a release.

Out in the hallway, he noticed her bedroom door was cracked open. She normally immediately shut and locked it, but this time, she hadn't. He crept down the darkened hallway, his footsteps quiet on the carpet. Her door was open enough for him to see her leaning back in her desk chair, her dress hiked up around her waist.

She sat bare, legs out wide, and he could see how wet she was even from out in the hall. Sunday was using some toy that kind of looked like a severed hand, but he wasn't surprised at the odd choice of accessories this girl used. She was certainly *very* odd.

Auggie had stood out in the hallway, his breath quickening as he watched that toy finger fuck Sunday into an intense orgasm. He wanted to be those fingers. To feel the inside of her squeeze around him. He wanted her breaths blowing in his ear.

Auggie had to quickly stifle a groan when he watched Sunday squirt all over the hand that was shoved deep inside her. He walked quickly but quietly back to his room and shut his door. He heard her door open all the way, the hinges squeaking, and heard her footsteps as they passed by his bedroom to head downstairs. She had paused slightly outside his door, and Auggie held his breath.

He willed his dick to calm down, wanting to follow her down to dinner just for the chance to get to smell her arousal. He quickly adjusted himself and opened his door. She was only a few steps down the hall, and she waited for him.

Auggie grinned at Sunday, noticing her flushed cheeks. His eyebrows raised slightly, and he took a deep inhale, "You smell delicious." He loved that her eyes widened in surprise when she looked up at him. He'd been envisioning those wide eyes looking up at him as she sat on her knees in front of him. He wanted to pull her back into her bedroom now to show her what she was doing to him.

Instead, they headed downstairs to dinner.

Dinner with Sunday's family and all their oddities was surprisingly refreshing. He felt like they existed in their own little world where they got to be their true, weird selves. They'd crafted a space where they didn't have to worry about the judgment of others. Not that Auggie hadn't noticed the way those girls had snickered when he and Sunday were in town.

People like that made Auggie's blood boil. He was the kind of person who knew this world needed weirdos. He knew this world would be a whole heck of a lot more boring without people like the Strange family.

Auggie loved that Sunday lived in her big, creepy mansion with so many members of her family. He loved that her dad was overly outgoing and liked to talk about the strange places he'd traveled to and the weird collectibles he picked up. He found it cool that her grandmama spoke this weird witchy chant before they all started eating and that it looked like her mother was stirring her tea with some kind of touchless spoon.

And in the middle of all of that was Sunday. The one member of the family, at least in his mind, that seemed to have the most connection to the outside world, albeit from the corner of her room. He'd noticed all the forensics books stacked on her desk and knew she was working to make a real difference for so many families by helping with all those cold cases.

He knew, without her even needing to tell him, that this

was where Sunday would always be. That she had allowed herself a connection to the outside world, but on her terms. He had sat and wondered this afternoon what staying here might feel like for him. Not that he'd been asked to. Not that Sunday even wanted to see more of him. But something simmered in his gut that it might be an option if he brought it up.

Auggie thought about everything that was waiting for him back home. A lifeless job. An empty apartment. His friend group was the only thing keeping him tied, and none of them seemed to care that he was currently missing. So, what if Auggie gave it all up? Even if staying here wasn't an option, what was stopping Auggie from packing it all up and leaving?

Absolutely nothing.

He looked up, feeling a weighted gaze on him, and locked eyes with Sunday. Sometimes, it felt like she could peer right into his mind. Auggie winked at her before bringing another forkful of the roasted chicken to his mouth.

Her eyes widened slightly, and that made Auggie smile. He liked unraveling her. He liked meeting her dark, blunt energy with his cheery one. He liked being the one to surprise Sunday.

Auggie would stay another night. He'd still been unable to get ahold of any of the guys; his messages had gone through, but no one had responded. He'd try again tomorrow. But maybe tonight, he'd try Sunday.

He wanted to see if what he thought was sparking between them was real or if it was all in his horny head. He wanted to kiss more than her knuckles, and he wanted to watch her cheeks flush in real time as he buried himself inside her.

Auggie's attention was brought again to Sunday as she cleared her throat and shifted in her seat. Could she hear his dirty thoughts? He tested it out by drawing up a detailed vision of exactly what he wanted to do with her in his mind. The entire time, he stared at her face.

Wanna play, Sunday? Auggie slid his hand up the back of her dress and felt bare skin under his fingers. He growled in her ear and gripped her tightly. He ripped her dress off and spun her around, holding onto her braids tightly in one hand and roughly squeezing her breasts with the other. He opened his palm and drugged it down her belly, heading further down until he reached her core. He could feel the heat radiating from it, and he covered the entire thing with his large hand, cupping her, lifting her slightly, and—

Sunday's cheeks were flushed, her silverware rattled as she set it down on her plate, and she looked at him with fire in her eyes. *Maybe she* could *read my thoughts.* She sucked on her bottom lip and paused to calm her breathing. Auggie wanted to lick that bottom lip.

After dinner, and when the rest of the family went into the sitting room for dessert, Sunday headed upstairs. So Auggie followed her. He caught up to her in the darkened hallway of the second floor. He backed her up against a wall, caging her in with his body.

"I wanted to see if you smelled just as good as you did

earlier when I watched you come at your desk." Auggie dipped his face down to her neck and took a breath.

Sunday gripped his wrists as they held her up against the wall, and he thought that maybe she was going to push him away. But instead, she took one of his hands and slid it up her dress, and Auggie was met with bare, wet skin.

She was *dripping*.

Auggie traced the moisture with two of his fingers, brought his hand back out, and slipped those fingers in his mouth. "You taste just as good as I thought you would."

Sunday's swollen lips parted, and he seized the opportunity to taste more of her. He gently placed his lips on hers, testing the waters. When she slipped her tongue past his teeth, he dove right in. Their mouths were warm as they blended in a clash of lips and teeth and tongues.

Auggie could feel himself growing hard in his pants. It was hard not to around Sunday. Her little, quiet, emo-girl personality did something for him. He wanted to make the quiet girl scream while she came on his cock.

Sensing a shift in Auggie, probably from reading his mind, Sunday ground into his bulge, and it was almost enough to make him come. He groaned in her ear and pulled himself off her. They stared at each other for a beat, panting.

"I would love to be inside you. Is that something you're up for?" Auggie asked before he could get his hopes up. He might have all these fantasies of fucking Sunday in every way imaginable, but she might have them.

He watched as she unbuttoned the top of her dress, her

eyes locked on his. He saw flashes of creamy skin, but he said, "I need to hear your words, Sunday. Talk to me."

Sunday kept unbuttoning her dress, widening the top part of the fabric enough to show him she wasn't wearing a bra either. He saw the peak of her nipple harden in the cool air.

"I want you to fuck me, August."

Sunday felt mildly guilty for allowing Auggie to follow her back to her bedroom, knowing she was about to beg him to fuck her brains out. The knowledge about his presence in her eternal life lay like a weapon inside her thoughts.

She was hoping that the magic wouldn't feel like she was tricking Auggie into staying. The rules of magic were strict, and no matter how many ways she could think of bending them, at the end of the day, it wouldn't let her.

But she knew, based on the bulge in Auggie's pants, that he wanted this as much as she did. And he'd let it slip out in the hallway that he'd watched her before dinner. When Cosa had fingered her so well, she'd squirted all over it. Sunday could only wonder what wild reasoning Auggie gave himself for what Cosa could be.

There was one *tiny* factor that might derail her plans with Auggie. The tiny factor was that even though she had entertained herself with Cosa and other toys, Sunday was, in fact, a virgin.

As the years had gone by and the Strange family became more and more reclusive, she had watched her chance of getting railed slip away. The town at the bottom of their hill had rapidly descended into a near ghost town, with the closest public school being over a half hour away. Given that and the fact that Sunday *hated* people, she wasn't set up for success in the virginity-losing department.

So, as she tugged Auggie by his t-shirt through her bedroom door and locked it, she hoped this wouldn't slow him down. Her room sat behind them in a flickering glow. Sunday's candle collection sat burning around the room, wax dripping down the edges.

Sunday backed up until her thighs hit the edge of her mattress and brought Auggie with her, his mouth never leaving hers. Now that she'd gotten a taste of him, she didn't want to let go. Her teeth captured his bottom lip, and she tugged. She smiled as he groaned against her mouth.

Sunday sat on the edge of the bed, her dress bunched up around her waist and her bare, wet pussy on display for Auggie. He pulled away from her mouth, leaving her lips swollen as he stepped back and assessed her. He wiped a thumb across the bottom of his lip and grinned.

Before Sunday could finish the dirty thought in her mind, Auggie gripped the sides of her dress and tugged it over her head, leaving her completely naked. His hands skirted down her body as he tugged her closer to the edge of the mattress.

Auggie made an approving growl in his throat and fell to his knees in front of her. The first swipe of his tongue at her core almost made her come undone. There was no feeling to compare this to. No toy that would mimic the warmth he brought between her legs. And when he shoved that tongue inside her, she gasped.

Sunday's legs hovered on either side of his face, and she dropped a hand to his head and threaded her fingers between his curls. She tugged him closer to her, and he growled into her core, the vibrations riding all the way up to her belly.

"Add your fingers," she huffed, "make me come."

Auggie listened. He slid two fingers between her folds and pumped as he continued to devour her with his mouth.

"Oh god, oh god," Sunday's breathing was ragged, "don't stop."

Auggie listened. He didn't change his pace or let up, and when his fingers finally flicked the sensitive part of her insides, she exploded all over his face. He looked up at her, his face glistening, with a devilish grin.

Sunday took a few seconds to catch her breath before she tugged at Auggie's shoulders to get him to stand, then she reached for the button on his pants. He sighed in relief as she slid the zipper down, freeing him from the confines of the material. Sunday looked up at Auggie, locked eyes with him, and tugged down his pants and boxers, revealing what was waiting for her inside.

She licked her lips hungrily when she took in what Auggie was working with. She wanted to taste him. She wanted to feel him in the back of her throat. She wanted him inside her. She wanted so many things when it came to Auggie.

Sunday had also never given a blow job. Not that she couldn't imagine what she needed to do, but she hoped she could provide as much pleasure as Auggie did for her. She wrapped her hand around the warmth of his cock and stroked it gently.

"You don't have to if you don't want to," Auggie said from above her, looking down with lust and admiration.

"I want to, I really want to." Sunday slipped her tongue out of her mouth to taste him. "I want you to fuck my face."

Auggie threw his head back and groaned, reached down, and gripped himself in his hand, tugging firmly. He guided his swollen cock to her mouth, and she opened greedily. He stroked himself a couple of times at the entrance of her mouth, letting her get used to his width.

Sunday adjusted her jaw and leaned forward a bit so he could slide in further. Auggie hissed as she took in more and more of him. She swirled her tongue against the length of him as he began to pull out and back in.

Auggie started off gently, getting Sunday used to the pressure of her mouth being open so wide. But when she gripped his backside, digging her nails in, he reached for the back of her head and pushed her down on him.

Sunday moaned as Auggie shoved himself deep in her mouth, tears stinging the corners of her eyes. This was exactly like he had envisioned. She had seen him dreaming up this scenario, and she was thrilled to be getting to do it in real life.

Sloppy sounds fill the room as Auggie thoroughly fucked

Sunday's face. She could hear him moaning, and suddenly, he pulled out of her mouth with a pop. "I don't want to come yet, and if you keep that up, I'm gonna come down your throat."

Sunday smiled up at him like she wouldn't mind but was happy for the chance to get to feel Auggie's thick cock between her legs. She scooted back on the bed and leaned back against her pile of pillows.

Auggie climbed up on the bed after her, a predatory grin on his face. God, she wanted him to wreck her. She wanted it to hurt; she wanted it to last forever; she wanted *him*.

"Do you have any condoms?" Auggie looked around for a nightstand drawer, but the only thing he'd find in there were about seven different vibrators.

"Uh, no, but it's fine, I won't get pregnant." Sunday didn't know how she knew, but she also trusted that the magic here would protect her.

Auggie looked at her curiously. "You have done this before, right?"

Sunday grinned sexily, hoping to distract him. "I've done lots of things before. I think you've seen me do one of those things already." She hoped reminding him about what he'd witnessed from the hallway earlier would remind him she was no prude. Just a virgin.

"Yeah, but have you had sex before?" Auggie leaned down and peppered kisses down her neck. "Have you had someone else's cock inside you before, Sunday?"

The way that Auggie was asking made her believe he wouldn't mind learning about her virginity. His tongue made a path between her breasts as he continued, "Will I get to be the first cock that's inside this pussy? I get the feeling you're a bit of a dirty girl, so I don't have any assumptions you're not ready, but I just wanna know, Sunday, am I the first guy to get to fuck you senseless?"

Sunday swallowed, her heart beating out of her chest and her arousal pooling between her legs. *Who was this guy?* "You will be my first, August. It's just you."

Auggie growled in her ear as he reached his hand down between her legs, dipping two fingers in to feel her wetness. "So ready for me already, Sunday. When I watched you with your toy before dinner, I almost came barging in here just to get a taste. I could smell you out in the hallway, and I almost couldn't help myself."

Auggie gently fingered her, getting her ready to take him. He added a second finger, then a third and she moaned, arching into his touch. "I need to get you ready for me, Sunday. I don't want it to hurt."

"I do," she said, and the way Auggie's eyes darkened had her breath quickening.

He sighed like he didn't know what to do with her, and maybe he didn't. Maybe Sunday should save him from himself and not let him tip over the edge with her. This was going to make it that much harder when he left.

But Sunday wasn't the kind of girl to fight *for* anything, so she certainly wouldn't let herself be the person who fought *against* anything, either. She angled her hips up to allow Auggie to shove his fingers deeper inside her, but she needed to feel more of him.

She whimpered, and he grinned. "Are you ready for me, Sunday?"

Sunday nodded, gripping her breasts in her own hands, and squeezing anything to satisfy the buzzing flooding through her body.

"You know I need to hear you," Auggie chastised her as he tapped his cock at her entrance, making her gasp.

"I'm ready, please, I *need* it." Sunday wasn't used to begging, but for this, she would.

Auggie pressed himself against her entrance, teasing her but also getting her used to the pressure. Sunday widened her legs out to her side and looked down at Auggie's thick cock as it began to slide inside. Her mouth was open as she watched herself greedily take him in.

They both released their breaths when Auggie finally settled all the way in. Sunday had felt nothing like this before. He felt hot inside her, and the pressure was immense, but she relaxed around him as he slid in and out.

Sunday's skin was slick with sweat as Auggie's hands slid around her waist to squeeze her as he fucked her. He gripped her hips as he drove himself into her over and over again.

"Oh my god, you feel so good around me, Sunday," Auggie said as he gripped her so tight, she expected she'd be bruised by tomorrow. He leaned around her while still inside and reached for the drawer of her nightstand. "I know you have a toy in here somewhere. I wanna make you come so hard on my cock."

He was about to see exactly what kind of toys she played with, but Sunday didn't have time to feel embarrassed. She wanted to come on him just as badly. Auggie leaned back with a small pink bullet vibrator in his hand and tested the power by tapping the button once.

It buzzed to life. Auggie slowed his thrusting down, widened her legs, and pressed the toy to her swollen clit. She nearly came undone immediately. Auggie pressed it harder into her and said, "I want you to strangle my cock, Sunday, do it for me. Come for me, baby."

Baby. Sunday *hated* pet names but from Auggie's lips? While he was demanding her to come? While he fucked her? She would allow it.

Auggie rotated his hips slightly and shifted the vibrator to just the right spot, and before she knew it, Sunday's toes were curling, and she'd exploded all over Auggie's cock, as he requested.

Once the final shockwaves left her system, Auggie slid out and said, "Turn around, get on your knees."

Sunday obeyed. She felt her orgasm dripping down her leg, and Auggie stared at her as she kneeled, ass up in the middle of the bed. She already missed his fullness. He scooted closer to her, pressed the tip of himself at her entrance, and asked, "Is this okay? Do you feel okay?"

"Yes, I feel great. Keep going." Her voice was shaky but confident as she leaned down on her elbows.

"God, you're perfect," Auggie whispered as he shoved his full length inside her. From this angle, he was touching new corners of her, and it felt fuller, deeper. She rocked back into him, craving more of him.

Auggie reached around, grabbed ahold of her braided

hair, and tugged on it gently. Her head raised back, and her throat exposed. With one hand tugging on her hair and the other hand overflowing with her breasts, Auggie fucked Sunday senseless.

She reached beside her to catch the vibrator as it rolled into her calf and turned it on. Sunday turned and reached back to urge Auggie to open his mouth so she could slide the vibrator in between his lips. Auggie wet it, his eyes never leaving hers.

She placed the wet vibrator over her nipples, causing them to come to stiff points, before dragging it down her belly and over her clit. Sunday bounced against Auggie, unable to stop herself from craving the friction. Sweat dripped down her back as goosebumps pricked her skin.

Sunday didn't stop the scream that came out of her mouth as she came around Auggie again. Before the orgasm could fade, Auggie slipped out of her and turned her around to lie on her back. He gripped his wet cock tightly and squeezed himself as he shot his come all over Sunday's belly.

They both laid in a sweaty, tangled, wet mess as they caught their breaths. Sunday was in a daze. Now that she had a taste and a feel for Auggie, she wasn't sure how she could ever live in a world without him. She wondered if he felt the same.

Auggie wasn't sure if he'd ever slept as good as he had last night. It had felt awkward for Auggie to get up and head down the hall to his bedroom right after he slid out of Sunday, but it felt just as awkward to assume she'd want him to spend the night in her bed. So Auggie had let her fall asleep next to him, her skin still glistening from their frenzied fuck, and he'd slipped out sometime after midnight.

This morning, he lay in the cool of the sheets of the bed wanting Sunday to wake with him between her legs. As he played out the vision in his mind, his hand around his waking cock, he thought he felt a small murmur of approval hum through his body.

The same feeling had been there at dinner when he couldn't help himself picturing all the things he wanted to do to Sunday, and it's what gave him the confidence to corner her in the hall. He had smelled her arousal as he followed her up the stairs, and he *knew* that she had wanted him just as badly.

It's what had given him the go-ahead to act a little out of the norm for him. He was pretty sure none of his past hookups would ever describe him as rough or firm in bed, but something about Sunday brought that out in him. Like he knew she wanted to be told what to do as long as being ravaged was one of them.

But Auggie didn't want to freak her out with how obsessed he was becoming with her, so he stopped squeezing his cock, took some deep breaths, and swung his legs out from under the sheets. He swore he heard a groan of disappointment from down the hall.

Auggie grinned and chuckled to himself as he threw on some shorts that he'd dug out of his weekend bag and a fresh shirt. Unzipping that bag made him remember that his friends still hadn't responded. At this point, Auggie was crossing his fingers that there was a blip in cell service from here to Lake Mellow and not that his friends didn't care what had happened to him.

Maybe he'd walk back down the hill today to try again. Auggie couldn't stay here forever. He hadn't thought to check to see if any of the Strange family owned a vehicle, but it might be time for desperate measures. Maybe Sunday could drive him into the next biggest town, and Auggie would have better luck with service there.

He had his hand raised, ready to knock on Sunday's door, when it creaked open. Auggie couldn't help but take her in as she stood there, with freshly braided hair, and a cute black dress that flowed out over her hips. Hips that he had surely bruised last night from his grip on them as he had pounded into her.

Sunday let Auggie continue staring, waiting for him as his eyes skirted up from her thighs to her hips, up to her breasts that peeked out slightly from the top of her scoop-necked dress. She didn't say anything as he leaned in, slid an arm around to her backside, and tugged her into his chest. He leaned down, and, without thinking, placed a soft kiss on her mouth.

"Good morning," he said.

"It is another day, yes," Sunday responded.

Auggie chuckled and pulled back, wanting instead to push her back into the room so he could see what she was wearing underneath this dress. He hoped it was nothing.

"I'm going to walk back into town this morning. Do you want to join me?" Auggie asked.

Sunday shrugged. "Sure."

They headed downstairs, made two coffees to-go, cream and sugar for Auggie, straight black for Sunday, and headed out into the summer morning heat.

"How are you feeling . . . you know . . . after last night?" Auggie asked as they walked side by side down the steps of the mansion.

"Fine," Sunday said.

"Fine? Like physically fine? You're not too sore? Or like fine, fine, it was just okay, fine?" Auggie nervously asked.

"Physically, I'm fine," Sunday answered, and it didn't do much to appease Auggie.

"Do I need to push you behind those rose bushes and make you suck my cock so you can get your morning fill?" Auggie asked, and he was only half joking. His cock hadn't softened since he woke up this morning.

"I wouldn't hate it," she said, taking a sip of her coffee like she was talking about the weather.

His eyes widened, turning dark, and he was officially rock hard now. Auggie glanced around them. A few gardeners were trimming hedges closer to the house, and Sunday's mother was having tea outside on one of the terraces. He leaned his shoulder into Sunday, guiding her around a curve of bushes that stood around four feet tall. He took her coffee and sat both of their tumblers on a flat part of the ground.

"Suck me off, Sunday," he said as he slipped himself out of his shorts and stroked, "and this time, I'm gonna come down your throat." The look on her face told Auggie that Sunday was just as into this as he was. She had a sly upturn of her mouth, not quite a grin, but her eyes shone with the challenge.

She fell to her knees without hesitation, the grass digging into her flesh, and gripped his cock tightly. She didn't tease him this morning, instead, she opened wide and took his entire cock in her mouth with one push.

Auggie let out a gasp-like moan and glanced around again. Everyone else was too far away to see them clearly. Not that he could (or would) do anything to stop this now. He took his hands, gripped the side of Sunday's head, and shoved himself deeper still until he heard a quiet gag as he reached the back of her throat.

The move didn't stop her; she widened her jaw slightly and managed to take more of him in her mouth as he thrusted in and out. God, she felt so good. Her mouth was so warm and wet and soft. Auggie wouldn't be able to last long. Especially knowing that they could get caught any moment. Something about it sent more blood to his cock and made him rock hard.

Sunday kept her mouth wrapped around him, spit dripped down her chin as she gripped her hands around his thighs and used him as leverage as she bobbed down his length. Auggie was only focused on the sight below him. He fixated on her dark eyes staring into his eyes as he got closer and closer to his climax. The wet sounds of her throat swallowing his length was music to his ears.

Right before he came, he swore he heard someone call his name in the distance. But the girl on her knees worshiping his cock kept his attention elsewhere. He groaned as he exploded deep inside Sunday's mouth and nearly passed out when she took her tongue and lapped up a drip of his come that had landed on her lips. Her lips were swollen, her neck flushed, and he'd bet money that she was soaking wet for him.

He wanted to lift the hem of her dress and slide his still hard cock inside her. He wanted to—

"Auggie! August, are you here?" There was the voice again; it was a lot closer now, and it sounded a lot like . . . Luke.

Auggie's brain was slow to catch up, especially after coming down from such an intense orgasm. So, he was surprised to see that, yes, it was Luke. And he was standing at the end of a row of rose bushes as Auggie stood there with his dick still inches away from Sunday's face as she sat back on her heels and caught her breath. Her hands were already trailing to find her center. She was ready for her own release.

"Auggie, what the fuck?" Luke was out of breath, having jogged up the rest of the hill. Auggie shoved his dick back in his shorts, and helped Sunday up to her feet, wiping the grass off her knees once she was standing. He swore he heard her huff out a sad groan at the interruption.

"Luke, how did you—how did you know I was here?" Auggie asked, out of breath and confused.

Luke's eyes darted from him to Sunday and back again as his brain put together the pieces of what he just saw. *Yes, it was his best friend getting his dick sucked by this random girl in the middle of a garden. Totally normal.* But even in his thoughts, Auggie knew Sunday wasn't some *random girl*.

Luke's eyes landed back on Auggie, "I've been trying to get ahold of you for two days! You haven't been responding to my texts, so I decided to drive the route you normally take to the lake today. I saw a bunch of red paint scratched on that tree down there and tire marks dug out in the gravel." Luke walked closer. "I thought maybe someone here might know where you went."

Luke glanced over at Sunday, who stood quietly off to the side. "I didn't know you'd . . ." Luke hesitated, finding the right words, "found someone to stay with."

"Luke, this is Sunday, Sunday, my friend Luke. He's one of the guys I was supposed to meet at the lake," Auggie introduced the two of them to try and fill the awkward silence.

"Hey, nice to meet you," Luke said with a small wave, but he was met only with silence from Sunday. "What happened, man?" Luke asked Auggie.

Auggie turned to Sunday and reached for one of her hands. "I'm gonna take a walk with Luke, okay? Meet you back at the house in a bit?"

"Sure," was all Sunday said as she picked up her coffee and walked back toward the house, a blank expression on her face.

Auggie grabbed his own coffee off the ground and turned to walk with Luke around the property. "Man, it's been a wild few days."

As Auggie and Luke walked through the hedges, he filled him in on everything that had happened since he crashed his car three nights ago, and how he had been trying to get ahold of people, but nothing ever went through.

"And, so what?" Luke asked as Auggie told him every-thing, "Now you just get your dick sucked by the emo girl who lives here or what?"

Auggie chuckled. "Man, Sunday is, I don't know, man, it's weird."

"Yeah, I'd say so," Luke said, "She looked like she was going to summon a curse for me just because I said 'hello.'"

Auggie wanted to defend Sunday, but he didn't know where to start. "Yeah, I mean, I don't know, I think there might be something there."

"Between you two?" Luke asked, his eyebrows raised.

Auggie shrugged, knowing it seemed ridiculous, but accepting that there was no way he could be making up what he felt around Sunday. "I know it's crazy, Luke, but you've seen how directionless I've felt the last few years since graduation. You all have so much going on. You *know* what you want out of life, and I've just felt . . . empty."

Auggie looked down at the dirt as he added, "Being around Sunday is exciting. There just seems to be this . . . energy . . . when I'm around her. I don't know how to describe it."

"I don't know, Aug, maybe she just sucks really good dick," Luke said in earnest.

"Yeah, maybe," Auggie said, even though deep down, he knew it wasn't just that. Although she was *good*.

"My car is here, just down the road. I think you should come back home, Aug." Luke stopped walking and turned to him, sympathy in his eyes.

"Yeah, maybe," Auggie sighed, and he swore he felt rage brewing down in his gut that he couldn't explain.

Auggie told Luke he'd meet him down the hill in an hour. He needed to pack his things and thank the Strange family for their hospitality. He also wanted a chance to say a proper goodbye to Sunday.

NINE

SUNDAY

Of course, he was leaving. Sunday knew what Auggie had decided before she even heard his footsteps walking up the stairs to the third floor. She had been served up visions of Auggie and Luke's conversation like they were specifically sent to mock and torture her.

She'd heard Auggie try and put into words whatever was going on between them. She had hoped he had been feeling the same unexplainable things she had been, but his confessions to Luke confirmed it. And even with that, he was leaving.

Even after getting down on her knees for him this morning, he was leaving. Not that she wouldn't have done that anyways. A part of her had known this whole time that getting Auggie to stay wasn't realistic. She would have not crossed that boundary last night. Or this morning. But she'd wanted to. No, that part she didn't regret.

However, Sunday had already brainstormed ways he could help her with her cases that were piling up. Between the two of them, her for the visions and him for the administrative portion, they could help many more people. She'd thought of how they could take over the entire third floor for themselves and how, tonight, she was going to ask him to stay in her bed all night.

None of that mattered now.

Because Auggie was leaving.

Auggie was leaving.

She'd slammed her bedroom door shut and kicked over her desk chair when she'd gotten the vision of Auggie telling Luke he'd meet him down the hill in an hour. He had hoped to come up here and say a *proper* goodbye. Well, fuck that.

If Auggie wanted to leave, he could leave without seeing her face again. She latched her door shut, drew her curtains closed, and crawled in between her covers, shoving her face into a pillow. Within minutes, there was a tap at her door.

Auggie.

Sunday didn't make a sound. She didn't even flinch when Auggie tried the knob, only to find it locked. She didn't react when she heard his voice from the other side of her door say, "Sunday, can we talk?"

She didn't respond even as Auggie said, "I'm gonna head out with Luke. I just wanted to say goodbye. I—"

She held her breath as Auggie paused, not wanting to risk the chance of him hearing her on the other side of the door.

"It was really great getting to know you, Sunday. I—

thank you for everything." She heard Auggie slide his hand down the panel of her door as he walked away.

Sunday didn't let out her breath until she heard the front door slam, and she knew, with that energy that'd been zapping through her veins for the last three days, that Auggie was gone.

Sunday didn't leave her room for the rest of the day. She didn't come out the next morning either. She knew someone had brought her some food because she could smell it from the other side of her door, but she ignored that, too.

This is why Sunday didn't let people in. This is why she didn't try to make friends, or, worse yet, lovers. Because they're never cut out for what she had to offer. They always wanted something else. Something less weird. Something less dark. Something less reclusive.

She had nothing normal to offer someone like Auggie. He had made the right call in leaving and never looking back. She couldn't blame him, but that didn't mean she needed to forgive him. As soon as Auggie had gotten to the bottom of the hill, the energy she'd been feeling between them went out like a light. She had wondered if Auggie had felt it, too.

The magic of the house must have been worried about her because by the second morning of not leaving her room, Sunday woke up to a platter of breakfast foods spread out over her bed and a carafe of steaming black coffee on her nightstand. She sat up in bed, reached for a piece of toast, and got some food in her belly. Even she couldn't stop the growl her stomach made as she took her first bite.

Sunday ended up devouring over two plates of breakfast

food before she leaned back against her pillows, exhausted from the energy it had taken her to chew and swallow. She fell into a restless sleep where she thought of only Auggie.

By the fourth evening of reclusiveness, Cosa had finally had enough. Sunday was never sure if it derived as much pleasure from their times together as she did, but she had to imagine that part of it liked it. She woke up with the moon glowing brightly through her curtains and Cosa resting on the corner of her bed.

Sunday gave it a small grin, and it took that as permission to scurry over closer to her. This was the longest she had gone without getting off in a while, so she welcomed her old friend. She leaned over to open the drawer of her nightstand to see what toys she wanted Cosa to use on her tonight, because tonight was about trying to forget about Auggie once and for all.

Sunday selected a small plug, her favorite bottle of aloe lube, a large dildo, and her bullet vibrator. She needed to be as distracted as possible tonight. She began to relax as Cosa rubbed her breasts gently and pinched her nipples between its fingers. She lubed up the plug and handed it to Cosa as she turned around and got on all fours, ass in the air.

Cosa applied gentle pressure at her backside, and she took a deep breath as it pushed it past the tight muscle and settled it into her. Sunday evened her breathing, getting used to the pressure and fullness before turning to lie on her back.

Sunday added squirts of lube to her pussy and the large dildo before sliding it up and down her center. Cosa took to slowly circling her clit, and when it pinched her, she gasped.

Cosa took hold of the dildo and slowly pushed it into Sunday, gently widening her. The feel of Auggie's warmth had been a lot better than this silicone knockoff, but it would have to do.

Sunday let out a long breath as Cosa slid the length of the toy inside her. Cosa pumped it in and out of her as she picked up her small vibrator and pressed the power button. Sunday was stuffed full as she added the vibration to her clit and tensed at the contact.

If only Auggie were here, she could have him stuff her mouth with his cock, then she'd be a happy woman. But Auggie wasn't here. He was never coming back. And so, in order to banish his existence from her memory, Sunday had Cosa fuck her hard with the dildo. It wasn't long before she found the right spot to add more pressure with her vibrator, and soon she was squirting over Cosa and the dildo as it sloppily fucked her.

She rolled over, feeling empty as Cosa slid the toy out of her, but also from the absence of Auggie. Cosa cleaned up Sunday and her toys, before letting her wallow alone in her pity.

After the fifth day of making her bed her permanent home, she finally made the journey downstairs, if only for coffee. The magic of the house was holding out on her and wouldn't keep enabling her reclusiveness by delivering her food and coffee, so if Sunday wanted her fix, she was going to have to get it herself.

Somehow, her family knew to keep clear of her, and she luckily didn't have to hear anyone say "good morning" to her while she grabbed a muffin and some coffee. Back in the comfort of her room, Sunday got to work. While Auggie was here, cases had piled up that she needed to immerse herself back into in order to summon the proper vision.

Diving back into the world of the dead is exactly what Sunday needed to distract herself. She had found that if she could read through a handful of files before bed, at least one of those would stand out to her in her dreams. A bit of information would be served up to her, making her shoot up in bed, and jot it down in her notebook. Sometimes, all she needed was one vision to find a missing connection that she knew would help the detectives solve the case. Other times, she needed to pore over the same case file night after night, collecting tiny bits of visions to form one big picture.

Tonight, Sunday picked three folders at random, crawled back up against her pillows, and started reading. The first was the case of an older man who was attacked in his home and robbed. He later died at the hospital, and after one flip through the file, she knew it was his grandson who'd killed him.

Apparently, there was a large sum of money being left to the grandson, and he'd gotten tired of waiting for it. It seemed he had a little bit of a gambling problem. It looked like the detectives weren't even looking into him seriously. Amateurs. Sunday just needed a vision of evidence she could anonymously report to the police department investigating his case and it would be solved.

The second file was a little trickier. This one was the case of a young mom who'd disappeared off the face of the earth while she was running some errands. The police didn't know if foul play was involved or if she'd run away on her own, leaving her family behind. Sunday noted a few details: the make and model of her car, what she was last seen wearing, and the face of her husband (it was always the husband). These details might help guide her visions tonight to deliver something helpful to her.

The final case Sunday had selected was much smaller, with little notes to go over. It was also the most recent, less than two weeks old. She didn't remember printing this one off, but there were endless cases on her desk, so one was bound to get lost in the shuffle.

Sunday's eyebrows furrowed as she read the details of the notes. Her eyes squinted at the scratchy scrawl of the detective who had written them.

Young man, mid-20s, never arrived at lakeside location where he was set to meet friends

Phone is pinging in Mellow Township, unable to locate

Wreckage spotted off Hallow Lane, airbags deployed

Body of August Miller found, deceased, behind steering wheel

DOA, family notified

Sunday dropped the file, her eyes widened, and her hands shook. *August Miller.* Was that Auggie's full name? It had to be. The likelihood of there being two guys named August who wrecked off Hallow Lane was nearly impossible—but *deceased?*

Auggie wasn't dead. At least Sunday didn't think so.

And if Auggie was dead then who had Luke been talking to? And where had Auggie gone? And why wasn't he back?

Questions swirled as she shuffled through her mind for any details that might clue her in on what the hell was going on. How could Auggie be *dead*? She had smelled him, felt him, he'd come down her throat for fuck's sake, and she had *tasted* him. She had felt the coarseness of his hair as she had tangled her hands in his curls.

Sunday knew she was odd, and she knew she was oddly obsessed with the dead, but that's when they were missing or *murder* victims, not ghosts that could finger her into oblivion. Even her family had talked to Auggie. Had they known he had been dead the entire time?

She needed to find Cousin Itta. She had much more experience in the occult than Sunday. Itta knew much more about how the immortal magic weaved through their family worked.

Maybe she would know what was going on with Auggie.

Perhaps she would know how to summon him back to Hallow Lane.

TEN
AUGUST

"You look different," Luke said for the fifth time since they left Mellow Township less than an hour ago. He looked over at Auggie in the passenger seat with concern. "Did you go to the hospital after your wreck?"

Auggie felt different. In fact, the further and further he got from the house on Hallow Lane, the less like himself he felt. Auggie took a deep breath before explaining to Luke, again, how everything went down.

"I hit the brakes, trying to avoid the tree that I must have just missed. After I hit it, the airbags deployed and made me a little dizzy, but I was fine. I opened my door and just walked up the hill toward the house, hoping to call one of you guys to come get me." Auggie shrugged. "I felt fine."

"Maybe you just need some greasy fast food. You look a little pale," Luke said, eyebrows still furrowed as they took in Auggie.

Luke took an exit a few miles down the road and pulled into a burger joint; the drive-thru had orange cones blocking it, so he had to park for them to go inside. August unbuckled his seat belt and tried to open the door handle, but nothing happened. It was like his hand couldn't grip the plastic, and it kept slipping from his grasp. *What the hell?*

"See what I mean?" Luke said, rolling his eyes. "You need nourishment."

Luke came around to his side to open the door for him, and Auggie slipped out of the seat, feeling slightly lightheaded.

Auggie followed Luke into the small lobby of the restaurant. The smell of fry oil and floor cleaner assaulted his senses as he stepped inside and walked up to the counter with Luke to order. Luke ordered a double bacon cheeseburger, and Auggie felt a pang in his stomach that must mean hunger, so he asked for the same thing.

The cashier didn't acknowledge him, so Luke said, "Make that two."

"You want two of the same things?" the pimply kid behind the counter asked.

Luke turned to look at Auggie, back at the cashier, and said, "Yeah, man, two."

"Okay, dude, whatever floats your boat," the kid responded, and Auggie's head hurt trying to figure out what could be so hard about ordering two burgers.

Auggie slid into a booth, rested his head on the cool laminate tabletop, and waited for Luke to fill up their sodas. He was so tired. Maybe the accident was worse than he thought, and he should've gone to the emergency room. Maybe he'd been walking around with an undiagnosed concussion for days. Why hadn't anyone in Sunday's family noticed?

It seemed like he had so much energy there, though. He recalled how great he felt inside that eerie old mansion. He felt more confident, stronger, more energized. But maybe that was the shock from the accident flooding his veins. Now that days had passed, and he wasn't around the lure of Sunday, reality was sinking in.

The cashier called their number, and Luke headed up to the counter to grab the trays of food. Auggie dug in and unwrapped the burger, hoping it could provide sustenance to make him feel better. The burger felt like ash in his mouth, and the fries felt mushy.

"This tastes like shit," Auggie said, pushing the tray away from him.

"Seriously?" Luke was halfway through with his burger, shoving a handful of fries in his mouth, and looked at Auggie like he had two heads.

"I'm gonna take you to the hospital, man. I don't know what was going on in that house back there, but you seem weird." Luke slurped his soda and added, "Did that chick put some weird spell on you or something?"

"Hey, man! Cut it out. You're creeping everyone out," the kid behind the register yelled to us from the counter.

Luke shook his head, unsure of what his problem was. But Auggie looked around and noticed curious stares, glances over shoulders, and a family scurrying out of the restaurant.

"Luke . . ." Auggie said quietly, "Something is going on."

"Yeah, this place is a hole-in-the-wall in the middle of some Podunk town." Luke stole some of Auggie's fries since he wasn't not eating them. "Not a lot of brain cells if ya know what I mean."

Auggie watched as a huge guy came from the back of the kitchen and stomped over to their table. "Okay, buddy, that's enough. We're gonna have to ask you to leave." The guy had grease stains down his white apron and smelled like cigarettes.

"What the hell, man?" Luke looked up at the guy. "We're just trying to eat our burgers, except you only made one that tastes good. Apparently, my friend here says this one tastes like shit." Luke pushed Auggie's tray toward the guy.

"Luke," Auggie warned; something didn't feel right.

"It's time to go, kid." The big, burly man grabbed Luke's arm and drug him out of the booth, leading him to the door. He didn't touch Auggie.

Auggie followed Luke as the guy tossed him out onto the sidewalk, shaking his head. He heard him whisper *fucking junkie* under his breath as he headed back inside.

"What the fuck was that about?" Luke yelled through the glass door and turned to Auggie, eyes wide.

"Come on, Luke, let's go." Auggie reached for his arm, leading him toward the car.

"Fucking weirdos." Luke kicked at a loose piece of gravel in the parking lot but followed him.

Auggie couldn't get the door open when they were back at the car, so Luke had to come over to his side to let him in, "Man, this feels too much like you're my boyfriend," Luke said. "We're gonna have to figure out what's wrong with you so you can get back to opening your own doors."

Auggie was getting an idea of what, exactly, could be going on with him, but it was so ludicrous, so ridiculous, there was no way it could be true. Because Auggie thought that, just maybe, he was dead.

Luke and Auggie sat in contemplative silence for another hour. Auggie wasn't sure what was going on in Luke's mind but his was certainly trying to piece together all the clues from the last few days. There were some facts that he knew to be true.

1. Sunday could most definitely see him, as could her family. But so could Luke.
2. Perhaps, the people in town couldn't, though. He remembered how odd the guy at the body shop had been when Sunday had to repeat Auggie's questions.
3. His body functioned enough to still get hard and definitely enough to finish inside Sunday (multiple times).
4. He didn't recall being that hungry over the last few days, and barely remembered eating any of the snacks he bought from the store.

Eventually Luke pulled off the highway to get gas. The

further Luke drove from Mellow Township and the mansion on Hallow Lane, the less Auggie felt whole. Luke pulled under the awning and parked his car next to pump number three.

"Luke, I—" Auggie said before Luke could get out of the car, "I don't feel great."

Luke turned to look at him, eyes wide and concern written all over his face. "I'm gonna get you to a hospital, man. Let me top off, then we're gonna find help."

Luke turned and exited the car before Auggie could stop him. Auggie stared at his hands in front of him from the passenger seat, his skin so pale it was nearly see-through. His breaths were shallow, and he felt nearly weightless, like he was on the brink of passing out, but couldn't get over the edge.

Luke slammed the door behind him and threw the car into drive before the seat belt even clicked in place. "I looked up a hospital," Luke said hurriedly. "There's one only a few miles down the highway."

"Luke . . ." Auggie didn't know how to broach the conversation with his friend. He didn't even know how Luke could *see* him right now.

"It's okay, buddy." Luke reached over to slap his knee, but his hand went right through the fabric of his jeans, his bone, muscle, and tendons, all the way through to the seat of the car. "What the fuck?" Luke swerved slightly while getting on the on-ramp, and a car honked as it whizzed by us.

Luke pulled his hand back and focused on getting the car back on the highway. Auggie was lightheaded and the space where Luke went through his knee felt icy and tingled.

"Okay, here it is!" Luke was bouncing in his seat at the sight of the hospital. Not that they were going to be able to do anything.

The tires screeched as Luke slammed on the brakes outside of the emergency room doors and he shouted, "Somebody help! My friend needs help!"

Auggie could only watch, unable to move his body, as Luke ran around to the passenger side and threw open the door. An emergency room team came jogging outside, stethoscopes swinging from their necks, eyes darting from Luke to the car and back again.

"Sir, are you hurt?" one of the nurses asked.

"No, it's my friend, he was in an accident three days ago." Luke bent down to help Auggie out of the chair, but he couldn't get a grip on him and instead left icy paths in the wake of his hands. "I think he's had a concussion or something, he says he doesn't feel right."

"Sir, how about you come on inside?" the nurse said gently to Luke.

"If you can just help me get my friend out of the car, I just—" Luke bent down to try and scoop Auggie up, but his hands only grasped air. "Auggie, help me out here, they're gonna think I'm crazy."

"Have you been drinking tonight, son?" Another nurse spoke up, his voice firm. Auggie noticed that the crowd of nurses had dwindled down to just him.

"Luke, I think we need to leave," Auggie said quietly, unable to muster the strength to speak up.

"No, Auggie, you need to be seen by a doctor and no one

here seems to care!" Luke's face was reddening, and his voice was shaky.

"Son, come inside and let's take a look." The nurse put a hand on Luke's shoulder to try and steer him inside, but Luke shook him off.

"If you can't help my friend, then there's no point in us coming inside." Luke turned away as the nurse tried to guide him in again and jumped back in the car. Auggie watched the worried look of the nurse fade to a pinpoint in the side mirror.

Luke's breathing had calmed a bit when he said, "I'll get you back to your place, once you're somewhere familiar you'll start to feel better. You just need some time."

Auggie knew that Luke's brain hadn't caught up with the reality that was sitting right next to him. That Auggie was dead, and he'd been talking to a ghost for the last few hours. So Auggie let him drive him to his apartment. He let him unlock the door for him and get him settled in bed. And he didn't argue when Luke made a makeshift bed on the couch and stayed to look over Auggie.

As a ghost, Auggie realized he couldn't sleep. Not that his body didn't feel drained and tired, but he could tell that his body shutting down for the night to rest wasn't really a thing for him anymore. And so, he walked around his apartment, even unnecessarily tiptoeing around Luke so he didn't wake him. Auggie needed more practice on being a proper ghost.

Auggie hovered his hand over the counter of his kitchen, taking in the apartment that was about to no longer be his.

His heart hurt for his parents who would inevitably show up to clean out his space. Auggie made an effort to hunt down any rogue condom packets so he could toss them in the trash and cleared his browser history before his mother accidentally came across them.

Auggie decided to fully tidy up before his parents arrived. He cleared off his small dining table. He tossed old restaurant menus, receipts, and plastic takeout silverware. As he dropped in another menu, this one to his favorite sushi place, a tiny scrap of paper fluttered to the floor. Auggie bent down to pick it up—an old fortune he took out of a cookie the night before he left for the lake.

Build a life where Sundays can be forever.

He remembers reading it as he finished his meal last week, rolling his eyes at the improbability of it. It was meant to encourage people to live a life that felt like the weekend. The day of rest everyone blows through in a hurry to get to the next time. But for him, it meant so much more.

He sighed now, taking another glance around his apartment. He was going to need to convince Luke to take him back.

Luckily for Auggie, but unluckily for Luke, all it took was four more days of fading more and more, now nearly totally see-through, and one ghostly jump scare for Luke to finally be convinced about Auggie's current condition.

Auggie had allowed Luke time to research his ailments.

He had allowed Luke time to test to see if anyone else could see Auggie or if it was still just him.

Auggie had even hung around as Luke exclaimed to his landlord that Auggie wasn't ready to give up his apartment yet.

Auggie's final straw was when he'd heard his parents on the phone with the landlord arranging a time for them to come down to pack up his things. His mom's tearful voice had bellowed through the speakerphone as the landlord stood outside the apartment door.

"What the fuck is going on, Aug?" Luke finally asked, his voice was shaking, as Auggie showed him, yet again, how his hand could go right through the arm of the couch.

"Luke," Auggie said, "I know this is going to sound crazy, and none of it makes sense, but," Auggie paused, eyes on Luke, "Luke, I think I'm dead."

Luke threw his head back and laughed. "What the hell, Auggie? You can't be serious?" He pushed a hand through his hair. "I can *see* you, though! You're right here!" Luke went to rest his hand on Auggie's shoulder but pulled his hand back instantly as it slipped through where his shoulder should've been.

"I don't know why you can see me, Luke; it seems like no one else can." Auggie's brain was trying to put all these mismatched puzzle pieces together, and it wasn't making sense.

"But the girl from that house could see you," Luke said. "She was sucking your dick when I found you, I saw it!"

Auggie shrugged. "I don't know man, maybe she can, like, see dead people or something."

They both stared off into the empty apartment, sounds of doors closing and water pipes groaning filled the empty space between them. Finally, Auggie spoke, "I think you need to take me back."

Luke's head quickly turned to Auggie. "Back to that creepy mansion? Why?"

Auggie shrugged. "I'm not really sure, but something about being there made me feel . . . less dead."

Tears puddled in the corners of Luke's eyes. "But why? I shouldn't be able to see you. If I can see you, maybe there's a chance you can—"

"No," Auggie cut him off, "I'm sorry, man. I—I think I died in that accident. I was just living in this weird in-between, waiting for you to find out and maybe for me to say goodbye, but I'm not actually here, Luke."

"Can't you just stay with me though?" Luke asked, tears streaming down his cheeks.

"I think there's something about that place that makes me exist more. I don't know what it is, but the longer I'm away, the more I feel myself disappear," Auggie answered softly.

Luke stared into Auggie's face, noticing the paler skin, the hollow of his eyes, the graying of his hair, and he nodded. "You just gonna live your ghost life getting your dick sucked by that emo girl, huh?"

"One could only hope that's how the afterlife is." Auggie chuckled and smiled at Luke. He would miss this. He would miss his best friend and the other guys he never got to say goodbye to. But there was nothing Auggie could do about it now.

Auggie felt hopeful for the first time in nearly a week. He was heading back to Hallow Lane. He was heading back to Sunday. He was only hoping the near week away wouldn't make whatever was happening to his body any worse.

"Did you know he was fucking *dead*?" Sunday yelled, her voice echoed off the glass panes of the conservatory her mother and Cousin Itta were having tea in. She couldn't believe she'd fucked a ghost and didn't even know it.

"No, that part of the vision wasn't clear when he first got here. The magic didn't reveal that he had already died." Cousin Itta sounded almost remorseful as she clarified the news for Sunday for the third time.

She sat, almost ethereal, in a near-sheer white gown, sipping tea next to Mother, the fleck of stardust shining in her iris, the tell-tale sign of her immortality on display. Cousin Itta would participate in these magical summoning ceremonies at night and into the early morning hours. After each ceremony, she seemed to glow more, her blonde hair shiny against skin that seemed to sparkle. But the glow of the stardust in her eye never disappeared.

Sunday had been content all this time, knowing that her mother and cousin were much more in tune with the magic of their family than she was. But now she was livid. She had been duped, tricked into *liking* this human, only to have him actually be dead.

It was a joke. Cruel and ruthless.

"The magic means no harm, Sunday," her Mother's calm voice spoke up. "There has to be some intention here that we're not seeing."

"Your magic," Sunday's voice was full of venom, "can go fuck itself." She turned on her heel and left the women behind her.

She tightened her fists and clenched her teeth as she stomped out of the room and up the stairs to her bedroom. The picture frames in the hall clattered against the wall as she slammed her door shut. Why was the magic so ruthless? Why would they tantalize her with someone that she *actually* started to care for, only to pull the rug out from under her?

Sunday shoved her hands across her desk, sending files, papers, and books flying to the floor. A rumble of thunder sounded in the distance, and she was pleased. Bring on the storm. She wouldn't mind the weather raging with her.

She didn't even understand why she was *truly* upset. What did Sunday think would have happened even if Auggie hadn't been dead? Had she truly expected a guy like him to want to stick around a place like Hallow Lane?

People like Auggie didn't *end up* with people like Sunday. No, guys like Auggie found people like her interesting, mysterious, and maybe a little sexy but weird. Guys like

Auggie only wanted to fuck girls like Sunday so they could have a story about that one time they made the emo girl come.

So even if Auggie hadn't been dead, he would've never been hers.

Sunday's mistake was allowing her brain to envision a world with Auggie. She had conjured up a false reality. And she needed to get used to the fact that it would never come to life.

Luke must have been sent here by the magic to retrieve Auggie. He must have stayed too long in the in-between, and the magic forced him to move through. Poor Luke was probably still convinced he was taking his best friend home. Sunday wondered when Luke would realize he was talking to a ghost.

Sunday paced the floor of her bedroom as the storm picked up outside. Rain shattered against the glass, wind howled through the trees, and lightning blasted over the sky. There was an energy brewing outside, and she could feel it.

It was making the hair on Sunday's arm stand up, and her breath felt sharp in her chest. She needed a distraction. Something in her told her to wait, that something was coming, but she was tired of hoping.

She opened her bedroom door and looked up and down the hallway. Sunday spotted Cosa waiting for her on a console table outside her bedroom. She held open her door for it as it scurried inside. Sunday couldn't sit still and stop pacing, so Cosa did what it does best and distracted her without hesitation.

It climbed up her legs, burying itself in between her thighs as she paced in front of her bedroom window. The feeling that something was *coming* beat through her chest. As Sunday paced, she chewed on her lip, cursed the magic, and Cosa slipped a finger inside her.

She barely registered the touch with how distracted she was, but Cosa keeps its pace. It was in no rush tonight. It was only there to distract her. It pushed one finger in and out of her as she finally laid back, mind whirling, on the small sofa that sat in front of her window.

Sunday's breath calmed as Cosa's work started to take effect. A zap of energy deep in her belly caused her to turn her head toward the window. Cosa slid out of her so she could lean over the edge of the sofa, peering through the leaded windowpanes. Her eyes squinted, trying to look through the streaks of water flowing down the glass.

Was that movement she saw?

A car door slamming startled her, and she left her bedroom to investigate. She knew Cosa would wait for her in her room to resume its work when she got back. Sunday could hear the storm raging even louder as she made her way down the flights of stairs and to the front door.

She hadn't even reached the bottom steps when the front door swung open, the sound of the storm whooshing into the house. She looked around, and no one else was there. Her family had seemingly all disappeared for the night. Whoever was waiting for her on the other side, she would need to deal with alone.

A flash of lightning illuminated the silhouette standing at her door, and Sunday froze.

Auggie.

When he pushed the door shut behind him, the storm continued outside, but the sound was cut off like a vacuum seal. His curls were wet from being out in the rain, but he was here. He was standing in front of her like a living, breathing human being, but Sunday knew he was not.

"You're dead," she said as a greeting.

"I am." Auggie chuckled, his face already feeling warmer being here. "I just found out. Turns out I'm less dead"—he looked down at his body, seemingly pleased with how he looked—"when I'm here."

"Less dead?" Sunday asked.

"Yeah." Auggie shrugged. "I can't explain it, but I feel more alive, more real when I'm here."

"But Luke was able to see you," Sunday said.

"Yeah," Auggie looked pained, "I think Luke was able to find me so he could say goodbye and tell my parents what happened. I felt myself disappearing the further he drove." Auggie took a step closer to Sunday. "So I asked him to bring me back."

Sunday glared up at him. "But you left."

A look of sorrow flashed over his face. "Yeah, I'm sorry. I was . . . confused."

"I don't know what's going on, Sunday," Auggie continued, "but if it's okay with you and your family, of course, I would love to stay here. I can sleep outside for all I care. I just"—he looked around the house—"feel more complete here. And something tells me that maybe you've been wanting me to stay, too."

Sunday said nothing as Auggie took a step closer and added, "If it's okay with you, I'd like to stay . . . with you. I think that maybe you're a big part of why I've felt so great the last few days." Auggie looked up at her, brows furrowed, waiting for her response. "I'm sorry I didn't know I was dead, Sunday."

He finally reached Sunday, and his hands trailed up her arms. She could feel him as if he were, in fact, a living, breathing human. She could smell him, rain, and the smell of greasy fast-food clinging to his clothes, as if he were fully living. She wondered whether he would still feel real if she touched him.

Sunday had mourned the idea of August. She had already started getting through the phases of letting him go, and yet here he was. Begging her to stay. Making her insides feel electric again.

She kept her arms at her sides as Auggie took inventory of her, seemingly cataloging every inch of her skin. Sunday didn't stop him as he slid a hand up her thigh beneath the hem of her dress. His fingers touched her inner thighs, sliding through her middle, and she gasped, bending over at the waist, unable to hold herself up completely.

"Already wet for me, huh?" He groaned into her ear, "Have you missed me that much, or have you been playing with your little toy, wishing it was me?"

She *had* missed him. She *had* wished it was his stiff cock inside her instead of her toy. She *had* missed the way he had filled her. Stretched her. Fucked her.

Her breath hitched as Auggie shoved two fingers deep inside her pussy and said, "God, I missed this. Did you miss me, Sunday? Have you missed how I made you come?"

And she did.

She ground herself once into his hand, then pushed off him, eyes full of desire, and turned to make her way upstairs, confident that Auggie would follow. He caught her waist at the turn in the stairs on the second floor and pushed himself against her backside. She could feel his hardness through his jeans. Sunday wasn't sure how ghosts got so hard, but she wouldn't let the thought ruin the moment.

She almost allowed Auggie to take her right then and there, but she pushed on and climbed the last two flights of stairs to reach the third floor. Sunday pushed open the door of her bedroom and dragged Auggie inside. Both of their eyes were wild, their breaths came out in pants.

His rain-soaked clothes stuck to him as she tried to pull his shirt over his head, but she was *very* pleased to note that he still felt the same. The hardness of his chest was still firm underneath her palm. The coarseness of his hair was still rough under her fingertips. The salt of his skin was still tangy as she licked the fingers he just had inside her.

Auggie groaned as he gripped the hem of her dress and dragged it over her head, leaving her bare, chest heaving, in front of him. He assessed every inch of her skin in approval. He grazed his thumb over his bottom lip like he was about to devour her, and she hoped that he did.

There was a new energy zapping around the room, and the wick of all of Sunday's candles flickered and swayed from an invisible breeze. She knew that as soon as they came together, they wouldn't be able to pull apart.

"There's something you should meet first," Sunday said, as she broke her stare from Auggie.

His eyebrows raised in curiosity as he nodded, "Okay, show me."

"I'll remind you not to judge me because you are, in fact, dead, so what could get weirder than that?" Sunday said, a little nervously.

Auggie put a hand to his chest like he was being sworn in. "I promise I won't judge."

She walked past Auggie, over to her desk, and stood next to Cosa. She pointed at it when she said, "This is Cosa, my . . ."

"Your toy," Auggie finished for her.

"Yeah," Sunday agreed.

"I saw you using it from the hallway, remember?" Auggie said.

"Yeah, but it's not like a regular toy," Sunday said. And she looked at Cosa. It took her cue and scuttled across her desk on its fingertips.

"Oh, it moves. Is it, like, real?" Auggie asked.

"Are you?" she countered.

"Touché." Auggie laughed, and his voice turned dark as he said, "Show me how it works."

Auggie sat on the edge of her bed and nodded at Sunday to sit in her desk chair. Her eyes didn't leave his face as she rested her bare ass on the seat and spread her legs out wide. She heard a sharp inhale from Auggie as she bared her wet pussy for him.

Cosa wasn't shy with a stranger in the room and headed toward her mouth. Auggie's eyes tracked its movements as it slipped two fingers past her lips and into her mouth, dipping them in and out, getting them wet. Auggie slipped off his shirt and damp jeans, leaving him in only his boxers with his cock straining against the fabric, and sat on the edge of her bed.

Cosa moved to her breasts, kneading them with wet fingers and pinched her nipples. Sunday's breasts felt heavy and full as she watched Auggie slip a hand past the hem of his boxers and stroke himself.

"Show me," she said. And Auggie listened. He slipped off his boxers, revealing his rock-hard cock. Sunday licked her lips.

Auggie noticed and chuckled. "Soon, baby. I want to watch Cosa make you squirt all over your chair."

Cosa slid down to her thighs, its fingers now glistened with her spit, and trailed one of them up her wet middle. Sunday let out a gasp and rolled her head back; her legs widened subconsciously.

Cosa pushed one finger, then another, past her entrance and settled deep inside her, hooking them in the spot it knows she loves. The sounds of Auggie stroking himself filled the air and almost made Sunday come on the spot. Cosa pumped into her faster and pressed its palm into her clit.

She moaned, unable to hold back for much longer; she

knew she was close. Auggie stood, hand still tugging his cock, and walked closer to her. As Cosa finger fucked Sunday, Auggie stroked his cock right by her face, almost close enough for her to taste.

And as Sunday exploded squirting all over Cosa and her chair, Auggie shot his release all over her chest. Their breaths came out in heaves as Cosa slid out of her, and Auggie said, "On the bed, now. Cosa, you too. Sunday," he said, as he scooped her up and tossed her back on her mattress, "we're all about to have *a lot* of fun."

TWELVE

SUNDAY

Sunday swore she saw lights burst around her room as she came in front of Auggie. The delirium of having him back here must have gone to her head. She lifted herself off her desk chair and crawled onto the mattress. She yelped as Auggie smacked his palm against her bare cheek.

Sunday liked it when Auggie took the lead. She liked it when he told her what to do and worked to wring out all the pleasure he could from deep inside her. Sunday didn't feel like the odd woman out around Auggie. How could she? She was about to fuck a ghost for goodness' sake. *Again.*

She moaned as Auggie gripped her hips tightly and only gasped once as he brought his face down to her core, shoving his tongue down her slit from behind. When he touched her, her skin was covered in goosebumps. Was it like this the first time?

"I guess we never really needed to worry about getting you pregnant, huh?" Auggie said from behind her.

"Nope," Sunday said through gritted teeth; the feel of Auggie's tongue circling her tight muscle had her thighs shaking already.

"Does that bother you?" Auggie asked, "That I can't get you pregnant?"

"Fuck no, children spawn from the depths of Hell," Sunday said. "I have no interest in them."

Auggie chuckled as he continued to feast on her from behind. "Cosa, come here."

Sunday turned her cheek and glanced behind her to watch as Cosa scurried over to Auggie and hopped up on her back. She startled from the tickle of its fingers as they pressed into her cheeks as it lowered.

"Yeah, right there," Auggie's voice was deep and rough like he was in a trance.

She felt something cold trickle down in between her cheeks and then slight pressure at her backside. Cosa pressed a finger into the tight muscle, and Sunday hissed.

"Relax, baby." Auggie massaged her cheeks, spreading her wide.

Sunday took a deep breath and relaxed as Cosa slid his finger past her tightness and settled into her. With Cosa at her backside, slowly sliding in and out, Auggie moved his mouth back down to her core, and she was in heaven. She rocked back on his face, craving friction, and luckily for her, Auggie listened.

As Auggie raised up, Sunday felt him slide his length through her wet middle, coating him with her arousal, "Spread your knees."

Sunday loved it when he directed her, so she listened, scooting her knees out wide on the mattress. The shift in movement caused Cosa to settle deeper and she couldn't help the moan that slipped from her mouth.

"Do you like that, baby? Do you like Cosa fucking your ass when I'm about to shove into that pussy?" Auggie tapped himself at her entrance, and she was ready to swallow him whole.

"Mmm, ye—" It was all Sunday could get out before Auggie shoved himself inside her, settling in deep.

"Oh, fuck, Sunday," Auggie said through gritted teeth as he slowly moved inside her.

Her skin was covered in goosebumps and felt like it was on fire at the same time. She opened her eyes and saw her candles glow brighter and her curtains blow from an invisible breeze.

"Do you feel that Sunday?" Auggie asked he began to properly fuck her. "This is where I'm meant to be. This is where I belong."

Sunday raised herself up on her elbows so she could get some leverage as she started to push herself back onto Auggie. He wasn't the only one who could control the pace. The sounds of Auggie's thighs smacking her cheeks filled the air as she continued to be filled by him and Cosa.

Sweat glided down her back as this weird energy continued flowing around the room. It was almost as if another presence was here with them, swirling around the room, around them as they fucked. A part of Sunday was worried this was the afterlife coming for Auggie. Maybe he got to come here to give her one final fucking before he was going to be called to the other side.

"I want to see you." Sunday turned back to Auggie. "I want to turn around." If this was, in fact, her last time with Auggie, she wanted to watch him as he came inside her. She wanted to see his brows furrow as he found his home between her legs.

Both Cosa and Auggie slid out of Sunday, and she directed Auggie to lie back against her pillows. She straddled his legs as she lowered herself down. Auggie's hands cupped her breasts and pinched her nipples as she lifted and lowered herself onto him. There was an undeniable presence in the room now.

Sunday watched as a foggy swirl of air curled around her and Auggie, dancing over their skin. She ignored it as she leaned her chest toward Auggie's face, and he took one of her nipples in his mouth. The swirl found its way in between them, and the cool air somehow warmed Sunday's skin.

"What is this?" Auggie asked as he trailed one hand through the fog.

"I don't know," Sunday admitted, "I'm afraid you might be leaving."

"I don't feel like I'm leaving," Auggie said, his mouth finding hers as his fingers cupped her chin, "For a dead person, I feel about as solid as I've ever felt."

Auggie slid his hand from her chin and gently gripped her throat as his other hand tweaked her nipple. The pressure and the pain caused a fury inside Sunday, and she shoved herself deep on his cock. Auggie lifted his hips up to meet her, and a moan left her mouth, vibrating against his palm.

He didn't let up. Auggie continued to lift his hips, impaling her sharply with every thrust. They were both almost covered in the fog now. She cried out as Cosa reached a clean finger to rub her clit as she kept riding Auggie. Sunday was dripping as she came again, this time all over Auggie. He followed her, seconds later, with his own release, shooting it deep inside her.

And as they both came, the fog around them shifted colors and flashed with a bright golden light. It was as if all the sky's stars had landed in Sunday's bedroom. Flecks of stardust littered her and Auggie's skin as they stayed connected, coming down from their highs. She reached out to touch the fog, the weightless feel of it resting in her palm.

She looked down at Auggie, pleasantly surprised to see him still beneath her. "See?" he said. "I told you I wasn't going anywhere."

Sunday's eyes took in Auggie beneath her, and her brows rose as soon as she spotted it. Her hands cupped his face as she stared into his eyes. In his left eye, in the far corner, was a speck of stardust. She lifted off him, feeling him drip down her inner thigh, but she didn't care. She needed to look in the mirror.

She rushed into her bathroom, leaned against her sink, and put her face inches away from the glass. Sunday actually smiled as soon as she saw the light catch on something shiny in her eye. They had been marked with the sign of the immortal. Both a human and a ghost have now been chosen to live an eternal life. *Together.*

Auggie walked in behind her, "Is everything okay? What was that fog?"

Sunday turned to him. "You told me you felt more alive here than anywhere else, right?"

Auggie nodded, "Yeah . . ."

"Well, good," Sunday said, "because that fog just made us both immortal, so I think that you might be stuck with me."

Auggie's brows furrowed. "But I was already dead."

Sunday shrugged. "I think you still *are*, technically. You just don't have to move on into the afterlife. You can stay here with me, and we can still see each other. I'm pretty sure my family will be able to see you, too."

Auggie tilted his chin up in contemplation. Did he not want to stay? Was he coming here to say goodbye to her? Sunday hurried to fill the silence. "I mean, you don't *have* to stay here. I guess, you can always—"

A sly smile crossed Auggie's face, "Oh, I'm staying here. I was just thinking up all the ways I'd get to fuck you now that we have forever." He stepped closer to her and reached a hand between her thighs, fingers scooping up his come that had dripped down.

He shoved those fingers back inside her with a growl. "This belongs in here." Auggie slid those fingers out and slipped them in her gaping mouth, "Or in here." Sunday licked his fingers clean, her eyes never leaving the speck of stardust in his.

Auggie gently pushed Sunday back to the counter, the

cool marble edge cutting through her skin. He fell quickly to his knees, and before she could register what he was doing, he pushed his face in between her legs and used his tongue to clean her. He slipped his tongue inside her, scooping up both of their arousals into his mouth and swallowing. Her hands were in his hair as he hummed into her core.

Sunday threw her head back as Auggie unapologetically devoured her. She couldn't believe that this man was hers for eternity. Finally, someone who didn't judge her brand of weirdness and, in fact, joined in with his own freaky tendencies. Auggie was her match in every way.

THIRTEEN
SUNDAY

The sound of a loud crow woke them, and Sunday wondered if she'd ever not be surprised that he was still here, choosing to be with her.

The two of them eventually ventured out of her room, finally needing fuel; well, Sunday did; Auggie was still, in fact, a ghost. Sunday's family sat waiting for them at the long, wooden dining table, a breakfast feast spread out before them. Auggie ran a hand through his curls, trying to tame them as they took their seats.

"Welcome to the Strange household," Sunday's cousin said to Auggie, raising her mug in a cheer.

Auggie smiled and glanced around the table at the rest of her family. Luckily, they all seem pleased that he, a mere regular human, got picked by their family magic to become immortal.

"Your stardust is beautiful, dear," Sunday's mother said to her.

"It's a little annoying. I can see it out of the corner of my eye when the light catches it," Sunday said bluntly, but Auggie could tell, deep down, she was pleased.

"Of course, dear," her mother added, a knowing wink sent in Auggie's direction.

"You know," Cousin Itta said at the other end of the table, "now that you're both immortal, you're welcome to join in on the moonlight ceremonies whenever you want."

"What are those for?" Auggie asked.

Itta smiled as she said, "It's our way of giving thanks for the magic that allows us to live eternally. It's . . . a way to replenish the magic."

"Sounds fun," Auggie said, reaching for the coffee carafe to refill Sunday's mug.

"Sounds like too many people," Sunday said.

She grabbed a couple of slices of toast and devoured some bacon. She was worn out from last night's activities and wanted to be ready to go again as soon as she could. She figured she could give Auggie a tour of the rest of the house today since this was where he'd live now.

"Mother," Sunday asked, "I was wondering if Auggie and I could take over the rest of the third floor? So we could have some more space."

Her mother turned to her father, and they shared a look, having an entire conversation without uttering a word, until her father said, "Of course, my sweet girl. The floor is yours."

Auggie smiled at how Sunday's parents spoke to her. They ignored her stoic personality and blunt, sometimes rude comments, and covered her in love anyway. They chuckled at her morbidity and odd fascinations and allowed her to just be *her*.

After breakfast, Sunday took them back upstairs and showed him the other closed-off rooms on the third floor. Besides her bedroom, there were two other guest rooms with adjoining bathrooms, one of which Auggie had used in his previous stay, a small office, a dusty library, and a large room full of items under sheets.

Sunday stood in the library, tiny streams of light coming in from the closed shutters, with her hands on her hips. "I think we start here," she said.

Over the next few hours and days, Auggie and Sunday worked tirelessly to transform the once-abandoned rooms of the third floor into their sanctuaries. Now that they'd been turned immortal, it seemed like they had closer access to the magic and could even summon it when necessary.

Sunday and Auggie practiced by calling on the magic to help them clean the dusty rooms, and before long, the library sat shining in front of them. Walnut shelves lined three walls and were filled, floor to ceiling, with books and tchotchkes. Worn rugs lined layered on the hard-wood floor, and plush chairs, now clean, sat ready for them around a large fireplace. Large, leaded windows opened to the wooded backyard at the other end of the room.

The place was truly magical in every sense of the word.

Auggie walked over to the windows, the moonlight lighting up the backyard. Off in the distance, past the tree line and on the other side of the swamp, Auggie watched dancing firelight. Now, he knew it was Cousin Itta and other immortal friends replenishing the magic.

"Should we join the ceremony tonight?" Auggie asked, turning to Sunday.

"I don't want to," she said.

"I think we'll need to at some point, you know." Auggie walked over to Sunday, wrapping his arms around her waist.

Sunday groaned against him. "Not tonight."

He kissed the top of her head, tugged down her braids to tilt her head up to his, placed a kiss on her mouth, and said, "Okay, another night, then."

"I've always wanted this room to be fixed up," Sunday said, parting from Auggie and trailing a finger on the bookshelves. "It always feels like these stories come alive when I'm in here. Like they're all just sitting and watching my every move."

Auggie watched Sunday as she glanced up at the tall bookshelves in wonder.

"I know it's not possible," she continued, "but it feels like the characters and writers of all of these stories can see me." She turned to Auggie with a sly grin. "Do you think they can see me?"

August watched as Sunday lifted the hem of her dress over her head and tossed it on a chair, standing fully naked in front of him. What was it with this girl and her not wearing underwear underneath her dresses? *He couldn't get enough of it.*

Sunday walked through the room, fingers trailing over

bookshelves, chairs, and side tables. "Do you think they like watching, Auggie?"

Auggie's voice was rough as he answered, "I know I do." Sunday cupped her own breasts and slid her hands over her body. Auggie grew hard in his pants.

"Do you think they can see me when I do this?" Sunday asked as she dipped a finger in between her legs.

Auggie only nodded as his eyes followed her.

"Do you think they would like to watch as you fuck me?" Sunday whispered from across the room.

"I do," Auggie said, barely able to get out the words, his cock straining against his zipper.

"Do you think they would like to watch as you fuck me in the ass?" Sunday asked as she slid two of her fingers inside herself.

Auggie groaned, his mouth fell open in surprise. "Yes, I think they would like that very much."

Auggie was even more excited as he heard Cosa come into the room, the large, heavy doors groaning as they opened. He and Cosa had a mutually beneficial relationship. It was always there, ready to warm up Sunday or fill her up while Auggie was busy everywhere else on her body.

She sighed as she lay back on a soft rug in front of the fireplace, the magic working to start a fire for her. Cosa was on her in an instant. It craved her pussy as much as Auggie did. He watched her relax as it slid a finger inside her to wet itself. But it didn't stay there for long.

Sunday turned over on all fours, ass up in the air, and Auggie watched, enchanted, as Cosa slid a thick finger in her ass, getting her ready for him. Auggie got rid of his pants and tugged his cock out, the heat of him burning his hand.

He roamed his hands over Sunday's back as he watched Cosa spread her wide for him. She moaned into his touch and pushed herself back on him. Cosa slid out and used its clean fingers to go back to Sunday's pussy. Auggie was about to fill her up.

Auggie teased the tight muscle with his cock, her arousal dripping out of her. Between the sounds of Cosa fingering her, Auggie slipped in. Slowly past the tightness of her entrance and steady as he settled inside her. Sunday took a few deep breaths in between moans as she flexed around him. *Fuck she feels so good.*

Auggie and Cosa found a rhythm, and they both fucked Sunday gently at first, both sliding in and out with ease. "Can you feel them watching you, baby?" Auggie asked.

Sunday groaned beneath him but raised her head to look around and grinned slyly at the books like she could see their faces. She must have been more relaxed and used to his size because she pushed herself back on him, shoving him deeper in her ass, and he hissed at the tight pressure around his cock.

"Fuck me, Auggie," Sunday demanded beneath him, and he listened. Both he and Cosa picked up their pace. Cosa added another finger, and she moaned, sweat trickling down her back. Auggie could feel that she was close; her muscles were strangling his cock.

"Come for me, Sunday, come for your audience," Auggie said.

And, like a good girl, she listened. She screamed as she

exploded, her arousal soaking Cosa. Auggie grunted as he came deep in her ass, and as he slid out, he shoved his juices deep in her pussy, "You know where this belongs," he growled.

They both lay, out of breath, on the rug, sweat curling Auggie's hair. He scooped Sunday closer, wrapping an arm around her shoulders and trailing a finger down her skin. She settled into his chest with a sigh.

Auggie sat up, slid his arms underneath her limp body, and carried her to their bedroom, not bothering to put on his pants since they had the floor to themselves. The magic had his back and had drawn a hot bath for Sunday. Auggie carefully lowered her into the tub, and grabbed a washcloth from the shelf so he could clean her. He dipped the cloth in the water, rung it out, and rubbed her shoulders.

Sunday was loose and dazed in the tub, so Auggie did all the work for her. A cup of hot tea appeared on the counter, and Auggie handed it to her, holding the cup against her lips so she could drink. Once Auggie got her clean, he drained the tub and scooped her out, drying her off with a warm towel. He carried her tired body to the bed and laid her down.

Her eyes fluttered to him as he laid down next to her, and he grinned as the light of the candles grabbed onto the stardust in her eye, the one that matched his, and sparkled. "I love you," Auggie whispered.

He knew that it might be redundant or silly to acknowledge now, especially after the magic already decided they were to live together in eternity, but he needed to say it. It needed to be spoken out loud for her to hear, whether she wanted to say it back or not.

"I think I love you, too," Sunday whispered back, her voice hoarse.

Auggie grinned down at her and placed a kiss on the top of her forehead. "I definitely didn't expect this to be how my life would turn out, but I'm really glad to be here. With you," he said.

"It's because I let you fuck me in the ass, isn't it?" Sunday said bluntly in the darkness of the room, and Auggie's eyes darted down to her in concern, but they softened as he saw the humor in her eyes.

His dark girl. His weird girl. The one he didn't find until he had died. The one he didn't ever want to live without. And he wouldn't have to.

DECEMBER

AVAILABLE NOW

GABI SALAS

ITTA

Moonlight shone through the leaves and cast dancing shadows on the forest floor as Itta made her way around the flames. She still wore her white, sheer dress, but it would soon be shed. August and Sunday were somewhere in the woods, half watching the ceremony, half too busy fucking each other.

They hadn't joined a moonlight ceremony yet, but eventually they would. They made their way closer and closer to the center of it all over the summer, and she had hoped that this Winter Solstice would lure them the rest of the way.

Every full moon, Itta and other eternal lifers would head out, deep into the woods, and past the swamp for the ceremony. It was a way for them to give back to the magic and replenish the energy it spent on serving them. It was a way to say thanks for their eternal lives, but Itta knew that the magic was as horny as the rest of them.

The magic liked watching. And luckily for it, the eternal

lifers liked putting on a show. Itta and Sunday were the only Strange family members in this sector. Of course, there were thousands of them spread out over the world. Joining these moonlight sessions were members of other magical families called to these woods by the pull of the magic.

Itta had been called to be the ceremony leader years ago when she first came to live with her aunt and uncle. Itta hadn't planned on staying for as long as she had, but she liked it here. She didn't know if she'd spend her entire immortal life here, but for now, it was home. As the ceremony leader, it was her job to make sure there were enough attendees present—and playing their part—to replenish the magic.

Itta walked around the roaring fire in the center of their ceremony, guiding and encouraging members to take part in the evening's festivities. Tonight, we had a couple of first timers, and Itta could tell they were nervous. Although the magic made them inherently sexually open people, the moonlight ceremonies could still be awkward at first.

It wasn't every day that groups of people circled around a large bonfire and fucked each other's brains out. It wasn't every day that select people would be pleasured by the magic itself. Only on the evening of the full moon would the magic fully unleash itself and take various forms that enabled itself to bring a few guests to release.

Itta loved it when the magic took form. She loved watching the shapes it would take, sometimes a hand that would linger over breasts, sometimes a cock that would slide between someone's legs. Its foggy form would shift as it floated through the space, serving up added pleasure to those it chose.

She loved the power she held as she walked around the fire, watching others lose themselves to the lull of the night. Part of the magic that Itta held tonight was a calming one. She gave off this energy of calm confidence to nervous guests that enabled them to fully give themselves to the night. It wasn't trickery or coercion; everyone held onto the full capability to say no and for that to be honored.

Itta's gift was more about giving them the confidence they needed to get to fully be themselves and seek the pleasure that bubbled inside them. She stepped around a couple, trailed her arm over the man's shoulder, and locked eyes with the woman on his lap. Itta nodded at the woman and watched as she slid down to her knees.

The woman's eyes never left Itta's as she opened her mouth wide and took the man's hard cock in her mouth. Itta smiled, pleased at the woman, and continued on her walk around the ceremony. Itta grazed her fingers over a woman's shoulders and down to her breasts as another woman sat in front of her, tongue trailing down her middle. Itta could tell the woman was close, and with a pinch to her nipples, she helped send the woman over the edge.

The magic chuckled in Itta's ear and spoke in a voice that only she could hear. *You like to play, don't you, Itta?*

The voice of the magic was deep and rumbly, rolling through her body like thunder. Itta didn't know why she, and only she, could hear its voice, but she liked its company. She missed its voice when it wasn't around.

As Itta walked around the fire, she felt the magic tug at the string holding her dress closed and felt it flutter to her feet. *Ready to see me naked already?* She thought in her mind, confident the magic would hear her.

I'm always ready for that, my darling.

Itta smiled, the warmth of the magic's words in her mind. She and the magic had enjoyed teasing each other at these ceremonies, and although it disappeared in between moon cycles, sometimes she could feel it watching her.

The eyes of the ceremony guests skirted over Itta's body as she made her way through the group. Her creamy skin glowed in the moonlight, her long blonde hair curtained over the side of her face, and her plump breasts bounced gently as she walked.

There's not a person here who isn't thinking about fucking you right now.

The voice of the magic spoke through her mind, and Itta responded, *Including you?*

Itta felt a whisper of the magic trail down her spine, and she shivered. She felt the weight of what would be its arm wrap around her belly and slide down between her legs. Her eyes glazed as the fog took the shape of a hand and cupped her middle.

I would happily hold everyone down and force them to watch as I fucked you.

Itta hummed her approval as it slid a magical finger down her core, finding her soaked before it vanished. Itta couldn't hold back the moan of disappointment that escaped her throat.

The magic chuckled in her ear. *Soon, my darling, it's almost time.*

The fire crackled, and the trees blew gently in the wind, most likely conjured up from the magic, as Itta continued her journey around the group.

Join in, darling; they want to taste you.

Itta turned to a small group of guests who were spread out on a large blanket. A woman sat with her back turned to the man she was riding, her breasts bouncing roughly. Another man sat in front of her, rubbing her clit with his thumb. Itta kneeled on the blanket next to them, and the woman turned to her, lust in her eyes.

The woman's mouth was full, swollen from desire, and Itta wanted to feel those lips on hers. Itta leaned forward and slid her tongue on the woman's lips; the woman moaned into her mouth as Itta crashed their lips together and slid her tongue past her teeth.

The man in front of her used his other hand to feel Itta, gripping her breasts. She was so wound up from the evening that she gripped his wrist and guided it directly to her middle.

Put his fingers inside you, Itta.

And she listened. She lifted herself up slightly, mouth never leaving the woman's, so the man could bury his fingers in her. Itta reached for the woman's breasts, feeling them sit heavy in her hands. As the woman pounded herself on the man underneath her, her breath quickened, and Itta knew she was about to come.

You're not allowed to come yet, darling. Help her come, but you will need to wait. It's not time yet.

Itta groaned, but she knew that, in the end, it would be worth the wait. The magic always made her wait to come on ceremony nights. If she helped enough people find their own release while edging off her own, the magic would reward her.

Itta stilled the man's hand that was buried in her, so she didn't break the magic's rule and focused on the woman. Itta moved down to her breasts and popped a nipple in her mouth as the man pressed the pad of his thumb to her clit. The sensations must have done the trick because, within seconds, the woman was screaming out her release.

Itta placed a kiss on the man's cheek and stood to continue providing her gift to the rest of the guests.

Go stand in front of him, darling, he's been thinking about your pussy the whole evening.

She turned to see a man sitting on the edge of a log bench and another man down on the forest floor, sucking on his cock. The man caught her eye and grinned. Itta walked over to stand in front of him, and he took a deep inhale, his face shoved against her skin. She was soaking wet and was going to need to be filled soon.

It won't be much longer, Itta. Let him come while his tongue is inside you; it's all he wants.

Itta's hands trailed through the man's short-cropped hair, tugging his face to her core. He grinned into her belly and dipped his head down. Itta watched as his cock disappeared into the other man's mouth and gasped as she felt a warm, wet tongue lap her up. The man fucked her with his tongue and fingers, and Itta clenched around him.

Tsk, tsk, Itta, it's not your turn yet.

Itta had to pull away quickly, just as the man found his own release, grunting as he spread his arousal over his own stomach. She was getting dizzy and lightheaded, and if she didn't get to come soon, she was going to be very grumpy.

For the next few hours, Itta was edged and tortured by the magic. It directed her to various guests and instructed her on how to help them find their own release while pushing back her own. By the time the ceremony was winding down, she was sweaty, hungry, and annoyed.

Itta was saying goodbye to the last guest, reaching for her dress that still lay on the forest floor when she heard the magic.

Did you think I was going to leave you to fend for yourself, darling?

Itta huffed a long strand of hair out of her eyes. *You disappeared there at the end. I thought you had left.*

I wouldn't be able to leave even if I wanted to. The final part of the ceremony has yet to take place. The part that replenishes me the most. The magic's voice was thick with desire in her mind.

Why did you wait until everyone had left? Itta asked the magic.

Because, at my core, I am a greedy creature. Tonight, I wanted to get to watch you explode all to myself.

Itta shuddered at its promise. She wouldn't last long and would probably come at the magic's first contact. And because they had become so in tune with each other over the years, the magic knew exactly what to do to help her.

It shifted its form into a thick cock, with rigid veins and a wide tip. With one fluid motion, it slipped into Itta easily. It caught her forward fall with a soft form, like a pillow, and held her up as it fucked her. The cock that the magic shifted into was always the same, so she'd been able to get used to its girth over time. The first time she saw it, she had clenched nervously.

But it had taken its time getting her ready for him. Slowly stretching her with its finger forms and easing into her gently. But by now, she was ready. She'd be sore tomorrow, but she could handle it. So, she threw herself back onto it over and over.

Before long, she shuddered around it, her muscles squeezing tightly. She let out gasps of breath, finally exhausted from all her pent-up energy. The magic slid its cock out of her, its form wet from her arousal, and lifted her in its arms. It gathered her dress from the ground and carried her, floating on a mysterious fog, back to the mansion.

Itta vaguely remembered how the magic tucked her into bed and wiped her down with a warm cloth. She fell asleep in the softness of her bed, feeling content and happy.

ACKNOWLEDGMENTS

The story literally would not have come to life if it weren't for two things. One: a major case of writer's block. And Two: a *fabulous* book club group that I'm in. There I was, wasting time online, scrolling for a new read for Fall, when I started seeing a theme. Paranormal. Spooky. *Slutty.* And this is what came out of that.

I never planned on writing anything that involved magic, ghosts, psychic powers, or anything spooky, but here we are —and it was so fun to write! I am so thankful you chose to read it :)

Thank you, as always, to my incredible team. Kimberly: you edit like a rockstar and I'm so happy to have found you. Kandice and Debbie: y'all were the BEST (and fastest) Alpha readers to have ever existed in all the land. Your initial feedback is always so valued.

To the crew at rOOTS KC Plant Shop . . . I have no words. Me being in your shop that day was true happenstance. Your immediate generosity in offering to throw a party for this shop (with spooky cocktails and tarot readings!) is something that truly helped this come together in the big way it has. Y'all, I was planning on sneakily releasing this book and doing *nothing* for it. I just wanted to write it. I love you all so much—I AM A PLANT DADDY.

To my family—the ones who read my books and those that don't—I love you all so much! Thank you for supporting this wild and crazy adventure. To B, do you regret reading over my shoulder and seeing "fuck her face?" ;)

ABOUT THE AUTHOR

Gabi Salas, the mastermind behind sizzling contemporary romances, believes reading smut is feminist AF. She's the author of the debut series "The Prism Society," a solid one-handed read *wink*. Gabi resides in Kansas City with her husband, hilarious daughter, and a ridiculously cuddly cat named Pepper. When not crafting stories, she's  drowning in honey oat milk lattes, binging smutty novels, or dark and twisty murder podcasts. Connect at gabisalas.com

The Prism Society Series

The Prism Society

The Passion Almanac: Magical Meetings

December

9 798988 905622